NOW AND FOREVER QUEEN

WORLD OF CONSTELLINA
BOOK TWO

C. M. HANO

Now and Forever Queen
Constellina Book Two
Copyright © 2023 by C. M.HANO

Printed in the United States of America
First Printing, 2023
Paperback ISBN: 979-8-9-880107-0-8
Hardcover ISBN: 979-8-9880107-1-5
Barnes & Noble Hardcover ISBN: 979-8-3692217-9-2

Cover Design By: C. M. Hano
Edited by: Sue Allerton
Proofing by: Sue Allerton
Map Created By: V. M. Jaskerina (http://www.vmjaskiernia.com/)

CONTENTS

CHAPTER ONE 1

CHAPTER TWO 12

CHAPTER THREE 26

CHAPTER FOUR 35

CHAPTER FIVE 46

CHAPTER SIX 52

CHAPTER SEVEN 59

CHAPTER EIGHT 71

CHAPTER NINE 82

CHAPTER TEN 93

CHAPTER ELEVEN 104

CHAPTER TWELVE: 117

CHAPTER THIRTEEN 127

CHAPTER FOURTEEN 138

CHAPTER FIFTEEN 149

CHAPTER SIXTEEN 163

CHAPTER SEVENTEEN 175

CHAPTER EIGHTEEN 187

CHAPTER NINETEEN 201

CHAPTER TWENTY: 208

STAY IN TOUCH: 220

ACKNOWLEDGEMENTS 221

ALSO, BY C. M. HANO 222

DEDICATION

To Viviana, because we would both go into Locknite to
rescue one another

FOREWORD

This book is not suitable for any audience under the age
of 18. This book contains explicit language, graphic
violence, detailed sex scenes, and the mention of a past
rape. Kidnapping, torture, and death are also included in this
book. All sexual content is consensual between the Female
Main Character and Male Main Character.
Please do not read this book if you feel that any of this
content may trigger for you. I want all my readers to enjoy
this adventure to their fullest.

CHAPTER ONE

Gwen

With one foot in front of the other, I push forward into the Fields of Camillian. The glamor Alexxander placed on me never faltered, but knowing that I don't look like the real me makes my fists clench.

"Change me back," I demand as he scans the area behind us. Kalice City is far away, but you can't be too careful these days. My face is plastered all over the realm as the abducted princess, and Alexxander, well, he's accused of doing the crime. "Did you hear me?"

His head snaps in my direction, golden locks brushing against his brows as his own disguise slips away, revealing his true form. "Yes. But what's the rush, princess?"

I scoff, gesturing to my body. "I don't look like the real me. Change me back."

He moves closer, swallowing up the distance between us in two easy strides. My back hits the trunk of a tree as his hands land on my hips and his eyes bore into mine, a whisper of a breath between us. "Ask nicely."

I narrow my eyes, inwardly chastising myself for allowing him to come this close to me again. His ash and spice scent clouds my senses as his familiar touch ignites my skin. *Pull yourself together, Gwen.* In a split second, I palm my daggers. One pressed to his throat, the other against his cock. "You have no right to touch me, to demand politeness, to even breathe the same air as me." I gather the rest of my strength to say these next words with as much venom as his tongue had spewed in that courtroom. "The only reason you're here is that we need your help to break into Locknite. But if you ever touch me again, I will not hesitate to kill you."

The smirk on his face falls, his expression turning stoic as I feel it, the hum of magic as it encompasses my body. Like a loose glove, the glamor slips, and I feel the real like me again. "You're my mate, Gwen. I'll never stop trying to win you back."

"I'm not your mate, Alexxander. The sooner you accept that, the better. Back off." I wait for him to move, but he reaches up to tuck a loose curl behind my ear. A firm hand captures his wrist.

The scent of moonflower and ash overwhelms Alexxander's. "You heard her. Back off, brother."

Arthur, Alexxander's older brother, and twin.

His bright blue eyes look between the two of us, trying to solve some sort of puzzle that has presented itself. "Hmm. Aren't you two just the best of friends? You'll see my brother's true colors, Princess. And when you do, I'll be ready for you."

Alexxander backs away, his golden wings bursting to life before he takes flight, leaving nothing but dust particles and silence behind.

"You okay, Sunshine?" Arthur's question breaks through the beating in my ears. As I look at him, I reach out and touch the tip of his jagged ear.

"How did this happen?" It comes out as a whisper. My fingers, on their own accord, trail down the length of his ear, stubble along his jaw, and down the side of his neck. His breath hitches as our eyes lock for a second. I think I see that fire again, but he bats my hand away.

"We need to get moving. It's a long trek to Locknite and you're not ready yet. Besides, we still need to find a way across the sea." I watch as Arthur turns on his heel and saunters into the trees. We have no path to follow, but Alexxander can fly, and Arthur swears he knows the continent like the back of his hand. While I wasn't keen on trusting shifters before, these two showed up in my life, yet I'd say they're the best chance I have at saving not only Tori but also all of Constellina.

We walk in silence, the only noise being the crunching of fallen leaves beneath our boots. My mind races with questions as I remember the dreams I've been having.

His hand trailing up my thigh, grip on my throat tightening, and then...

"Stop." I berate myself, earning a concerned look from Arthur ahead of me. "Sorry, I thought I saw a viper."

"Didn't realize you were that concerned for my safety." He quips.

"I'm not," I shrug as I walk past him, clearing my head of all dreams to re-focus on the mission. His footfalls quicken as he catches up, our shoulders rubbing with each sway of our arms.

"That's right, you're just using me." He gripes.

3

"Just like *you're* using *me*?" I snap back.

"Don't sound so annoyed, Sunshine." His breath kisses my ear as he whispers, "Unless you want to use me for something other than gaining control of those powers?"

My heart thunders as the hair on the back of my neck raises in, not alarm, but desire. "Not a chance, Arthur. I'll never be stupid enough to fall into bed with a shifter again." I warn as I press forward. "Or any man."

I hear him chuckle behind me, and my stomach flutters. *I'm not attracted to Alexxander's brother. They're the same person. Gods! I need to get over this. What would Tori and Diliha do? I wish I could contact my friends. They would know what to do.*

A sudden gust of wind halts me in my tracks. Appearing just a few feet in front of us, golden dragon wings dissipate to reveal Alexxander in his human form, his black suit freshly pressed, hair trimmed into a high cut. My core heats. *Fuck, he smells good.*

"Easy, Princess. Your emotions are getting the best of you again." I follow his gaze to see pink lightning prickling along my fingertips.

Closing my eyes, I regain control again. "You left to go shower and change?" I ask, not hiding the bite in my tone.

"Why not?" He asks, cocking a brow.

I roll my eyes as I walk toward him. "Who wears a suit and dress shoes to a prison break?"

He stands his ground, hoping I'll let him reel me in. Only he is a fool. Stepping around him, I hold my breath, not wanting to allow myself to inhale his scent ever again. "I do. They're more than comfortable, and I can fight anything in them." I raise a brow. "Relax, Gwen. I also scouted ahead.

We should arrive in a small tree town soon. We can rest and recoup for the night there."

"Tree town? I didn't think anyone lived in this forest?" Arthur asks, but I continue to ignore them, thinking about what I can do to force myself to move on from this man.

The hairs on the back of my neck rise in warning, but it's far too late as thick rope snakes around my body in tight coils. The rope goes taut before jerking me sideways. My fingers reach for the hilts of my daggers, but the rope tightens further, cutting off my scream as it forces the air from my lungs where it holds my ribs in a vise. Pain lashes through my body, but I can't scream or move or even think. I just…stop.

"I would quit moving if I were you, Your Highness." A deep, masculine voice warns from behind me. He continues to speak as he moves into my line of sight. "These aren't just typical ropes. Nope. I got these infused with magic."

"If you value your life, you'll let me go." I snap.

He chuckles. The mask over his face reveals two brown eyes and dark brows. His broad shoulders are covered with a brown tunic and cut off at the seams, revealing two long arms, corded with muscle and tattoos. None of which I recognize. "There is a bounty for your pretty little head." He draws a knife, admiring its length like he's considering it as a purchase. "But, I don't intend on giving you up so easily."

"When I get free, you'll wish you'd have killed me." He laughs again before snapping his fingers. "Get her to her feet and remove any weapons she might have. I've got my bait. Now it's time to fish."

Fish? Bait?

Hands grab at me, hauling me to my feet as a smirk appears across my lips. "You think by capturing me, someone

5

will come to save me? You've lost your mind. I don't need saving."

"Looks to me like you do, Your Highness." He closes the distance between us. "I've heard a rumor that two powerful men want you. One of them is your mate, and the other is his brother." He leans closer to whisper in my ear. "What kind of mate would let his woman, a woman as beautiful as you, be taken prisoner by another man?"

"What kind of man thinks he can hold me prisoner?" I snarl as I reach for my power. I Think about all the things that make me happy, but when I open my eyes, my brow furrows as I see nothing. It didn't work.

"Move out." My captor barks, "We need to get back before the others come for her. I want to welcome our royal guests with a night they will remember for the rest of their lives. No matter how short it is."

Alexxander

"If you push too hard, she'll just keep fighting you." My brother's annoying voice rattles in my ears while Gwen's figure grows smaller with the distance she creates between us. Not just physically. "Stop pouting like a puppy whose favorite chew toy just got taken away from him."

I snap my gaze to my twin, snarling, "Watch your mouth. You may be older than me by two minutes, but I'm the one with his magic still intact." It's a harsh blow, but I've always had to put Arthur in his place. When we were kids, before our mother died, that's when we got along. But then she died, and our birthday came after...I rub my fingers through my fresh cut and shoulder past him.

C.M. HANO

The path ahead is unmarked territory. Within the forest, past the fields, is nothing but trees, animals, and peace. Once upon a time, there was a rumor of forest people, but that was proven wrong when no one ever came across them. On the other side of the trees is the vast Wall between my father's kingdom and Gwen's. The Wall of Illusion was put in place by Lettie and the other witches of the coven they created. I shudder at the thought of the traitorous bitch who nearly sunk her claws into me with her dark magic.

"What is your plan?" Arthur's voice cuts through my thoughts. I scan the area, inhaling the air just to mark her scent. "I mean when we get to Locknite? Are we going in there with fireballs? Or—"

"Shut up." I snap, halting us both in our steps. Arthur must have sensed it too, as a low rumble vibrates deep in his chest. "I don't smell her."

"I do." Before he even finishes speaking, he sprints forward, sending dust into the air in his wake. Following in his footsteps, I catch up until we're shoulder to shoulder, my wings itching to burst free and scout ahead. He stops suddenly, his eyes locked on something. I follow his gaze, and my spine locks up as I see Gwen held by ropes.. "Don't."

"We can't just let them take her." I bite back.

"Open your ears, brother. This is a trap for us." He states. "She's the bait, and I bet one of Outher's enemies sent these men after her. We'll covertly follow and wait until it is right to strike."

"She's my mate. She's already been taken from me twice before. I won't let it happen again." My wings burst from my back, fire igniting in my palms as my horns elongate in front of the crown of my head. I move forward, but before I

7

can take flight, something heavy slams into me, knocking me back ten feet. Trunks of trees shatter as my wings cut through them.

I don't gather my senses or breath in time before his hand is around my throat, pinning me to the ground. "I won't have you putting her life in even more danger and screwing this all up just because you're too foolish to realize that your dragon was mistaken." He bares his teeth at me, his talons threatening to penetrate my skin, "Gwenyfer is not your mate, and the sooner you come to terms with that, the better off we will all be. Pull yourself together, brother, or I will have to make good on my promise."

My eyebrows pinch together as I let his logical words cool my temper. "Get off me."

He releases his grip as my human form slips back into place. Offering me a hand, I wearily take it and let him pull me to my feet. Our eyes meet, but he smirks before letting go. "If we're going to save our little princess, we need to push aside our hate for one another and not let our emotions get in the way."

I straighten my suit as I stare at him while an overwhelming feeling takes hold of me.

"Alexxander," my dragon speaks to me. "Princess Gwenyfer of Sagittarian Court isn't our mate. I was mistaken."

"Mistaken?" I growl at him. "How does one make a mistake as major as this?"

His golden head falls in shame. "I have no answer for this. I felt it in my soul when we laid eyes on her. There is a fine line between an Unfated Mate and Fated Mate."

"You should've stayed dormant." I shut him out again, bringing myself back to the present.

"Are we agreed?" I look down at his outstretched hand, not knowing what I'm agreeing to, but saving Gwen is the right thing to do. Regardless of whose mate she is.

I grip his hand in mine and shake it. "Whatever it takes."

Arthur

My brother is pathetic.

The princess is sexy and fierce. I've had fantasies about her wrapping those lips around my cock as I drive into her while getting off in the shower, but I'm not some pussy whipped love struck teenager like he's been acting lately. I watched as those fae took her, knowing they were approaching us from a mile around. If he weren't so caught up with the idea of winning her over, he might've noticed them too.

It was my idea to follow their trail. Keeping enough distance away so they wouldn't spot us. I don't have access to all my dragon powers, but the ones I do have allow me to see a greater distance. hear things that a normal human wouldn't be able to detect. I watch as they make her walk up to a garden wall, clearly fake. To prove me right, the leader slices a dagger down the middle and a hole opens, letting them inside.

"Now we know how they get in." I say to Alexxander as his shoulder brushes against mine. "We can get her back just as easily as they took her."

"She's never going to forgive me after this." He shakes his head.

"Dude, nut up and shut the fuck up. I'm sick of your whining. You fucked up, own that shit. I've done terrible shit too, but you don't see me complaining about the consequences I've faced."

"No, you just kill." He replies.

"You're damn right. Because there's only one person in this entire world I can count on and that's me, myself, and I."

"You're wrong about that, brother." I give him a curious look. "Gwen. Once she decides to care about you, and for some ungodly reason she does, she'll move heaven and earth for you."

I don't find the words to argue with that statement because there are none. "That's why she's going to be the one to destroy Outher, not us." Gwenyfer has a fire in her I've never seen in a human before. Regardless of her being the first one I've ever known to have powers.

"And on that day, I'll be your friend again." Alexxander adds. "Because that means she'll be mine again. No one, not even my father, will be around to prevent that."

"You have high hopes." I whisper.

He digs in the pocket of his suit and pulls out a blue velvet box. I watch as he pops the lid open and shows me the diamond ring sitting in the center. "When this is all over, I'm going to make her my wife. She'll be my queen consort and within the next year, you'll have a niece or nephew to chase around."

I admire his vision of a happy life with her, but there's something about the image that makes me...angry. Like the idea of her choosing a marriage to him over me is unthinkable.

"Go for it, brother. Just don't ask me to stand by your side."

"Don't count on it. I know you'll be knee deep in pussy while I'm saying my vows." I chuckle to try to hide the hurt of the way he thinks of me. But more importantly, I wonder if that's what *she* thinks of me.

Alexxander and I decided to make a camp just a short

distance away from where the entrance was. I made up my mind about getting away from him to go investigate these fae further. I've never met one, and they're supposed to be extinct. This would be something interesting to tell my father. I'm still debating on whether I turn against Alexxander and the little princess, play their team for a while and report back to Outher.

My baby brother still needs to pay for betraying me all those years ago. Giving the woman he loves all the hope in the world and destroying it would just be perfect. First, I'll make her fall in love with me. As I watch my brother give in to the sleep, his body desperately needs, I sneak my way over to the wall. Pushing my hand again in the same exact spot. Nothing happens, not that I expected it to. I assume it's guarded by their magic and look for other spots within the wall.

The gods must favor me because the wall begins to open and a patrol of two of them come out. I covertly move when they separate and, one at a time, knock them unconscious, dragging the second one to the wall and using his handprint to open it. I quickly slip inside and find little miss Sunshine making her way down the path. Unguarded, unharmed, and apparently tipsy. I take a step. A branch cracks, and she stills.

CHAPTER TWO

Gwen

In chains again. Why does this keep happening to me?

My feet drag on while I try to desperately not move my upper body. I can feel the warmth of my blood dripping down from cuts caused by the rope wrapped around me. "You know, making me walk is causing the rope to tighten, too," I shout at my captor.

He chuckles. *I never knew I was this funny.*

"Oh, Your Highness, the ropes will not kill you unless I command them to. They tighten until they feel your blood, which I can smell, is already seeping into them."

"You're a shifter?" I ask.

"No." He states.

I get nothing more from him. My feet drag across the forest floor. I ventured into these woods thousands of times before, and never once, not even for a mere second, have I seen another human or shifter until now. Scanning my captors, I notice markings on each of their faces. Symbols from the old language that I can't recall. Studying history beyond our parents wasn't a priority for someone like me. Learning how to do as I was told and eat with the correct fork was deemed of the utmost importance.

It's a shame because learning more about this world could help me understand it better. Perhaps make me a better Queen when the time comes. If I get myself out of this one. I glance over my shoulder, thinking about my two companions and why they haven't made a scene. Alexxander would've taken this opportunity to save his 'mate'. I roll my eyes at the thought. "He's left you to be a prisoner, again," I mutter to myself. *Ease up, Sunshine. You know we're just waiting it out until we strike.* I imagine Arthur's smooth voice would say something like that. Or maybe it's just hope.

"Halt." The leader commands. I look on ahead, past the heads of the men as I try to catch a glimpse of where they are taking me. "Bring the prisoner forward."

Two very tall men jerk at the ropes, yanking me forward. I force myself to take a calming breath. I need to think, not allow myself to fall victim to fear. There would be no point in it, and if I am to die on this day, I want the scholars to note that Princess Gwenfyer of the Sagittarian Court was never afraid.

When I come up next to the leader, I peer over his shoulder but see nothing but overgrown branches and thorns. "When we get on the other side of this door, I'd advise you to keep that silver tongue of yours in check. Nefretiri doesn't take kindly to strangers. Especially royal ones."

"Why do you care? I'm your prisoner, remember?" I should kick myself in the mouth for saying that, but I couldn't help it.

He chuckles, although the face cloth makes it sound muffled. "And here I was told you had manners. I do not care what happens to you, but if you disrespect her, I'll ensure you never see outside of the prison cell we have reserved for you."

All humor vanishes from his eyes as they narrow with that very promise.

I nod my understanding.

Turning his back, he retrieves a dagger from inside his cloak and slices it down the middle of the branches. A golden light flashes until the branches move, the sound of crunching bark echoing as two doors open like the French doors leading into the courtroom back home. We step forward; the path changing from the fallen leaves to a cobblestone path. I blink twice as my eyes adjust to the bright light of the sun shining down on us with not a cloud in sight.

Different smells fill my nostrils as I try to pinpoint each one: cinnamon, peppermint, rosemary, and many more. A smile paints itself across my face, and I don't realize I am moving until the people stop walking to look at me. To them, I'm just a strange human bound with magical ropes who looks like a beggar. Each person has pointed ears. Their wardrobe reminds me of something from the past. Women in dresses and men in long pants tucked into knee-high leather boots with a V-neck tunic fitted to their torso.

Their eyes are all oval shaped with a golden iris and their skin is a deeper shade of brown than mine.

"So, this is the infamous princess." A woman's voice snaps my attention to the path ahead. I didn't realize we'd stepped

14

in front of an outside throne hall. Too busy soaking in all my new surroundings. "She's ugly."

"Excuse me?" I snap, to which my captor shoots daggers at me with his eyes.

"Emanuel, put her in her room. Provide her with clothing and a bath. I will not have her at my table looking or smelling like that." She orders. I know I should heed Emanuel's warning, but I'm not helpless enough to not stand up for myself.

"Nefretiri, was it?" I ask. "I understand you hate humankind. You think we're evil, and it's true, in some cases." I pause. "But we can also be loyal and honest. This man said that I was to be the bait for King Outher's sons. They will not come for me. I am nothing to them. King Outher will do whatever he can to take over the entire realm of Constellina, and if you are a wise leader, you will listen to what I have to say before you place your judgment on me."

There is nothing but the chirping of birds as everyone waits for her response.

She stands, her long ivory gown swaying with the movement of her hips as she approaches. The surrounding people instantly drop to their knees. Her eyes bore into mine as she reaches out with long, skinny fingers to grip my chin. It isn't painful, but hard enough for her to move my head from side to side as she assesses me. "You're a brave human. No one speaks to me like this, but I understand you are a ruler, too. If you think you can convince me that humans are not the evil of this world, I will hear your peace."

"Really?" I ask and her dark brow raises.

"Cooperate with Emanuel and we will discuss this evening."

"Okay. As long as these bindings can come off."

Her fingers release my chin. I watch as one of her long nails touches the rope. It instantly falls. My body relaxes as my lungs expand and my muscles scream in pain, causing a whimper to leave my lips. I stand my ground, although my knees buckle slightly as dizziness hits me.

"Take Gwenyfer to her room. No one is to disturb her, touch her, or harm her. For now, she is my guest." They don't give her a verbal reply, they just stand at attention before saluting her. A sigh of relief escapes. *Survive first, then escape.*

My body feels like it's been cut by a thousand knives. To make matters worse, they don't appear to have plumbing here. A pitcher, wooden tub, and oil are what I am given to clean myself with. When I was escorted here by my guard, Emanuel, I didn't think it would be as luxurious as the palace, but I figured it would have modernized things like a shower, toilet, and bed. Instead, there is a wooden bucket for bathing and a separate one for shitting. There is no bed but a spot on the floor with furs from several animals.

Wolves.

Bears.

Deer.

On the plus side, the warm water soothes my muscles, and the bleeding stopped. After I wash the lavender oil from my body, I stand and grab the cloth they gave me to dry with. It soaks through in seconds, not giving me enough material to thoroughly dry myself before having to get dressed.

I wrap my hair atop my head and walk out of the small alcove into the bedroom. A blue dress with long white sleeves is waiting for me alongside my boots and some stockings. "Too bad I don't have my daggers." I sigh while playing with the sleeves.

A long mirror attached to the door catches my attention. The frame is made from tree bark, but the glass looks real, and feels cool to the touch. I look at the cuts that line up and down my arms and torso. Emanuel left bandages for me and herbs to prevent infection. The cuts on my arms are superficial enough a simple bandage will work.

"This will not scar." I take a long bandage and carefully wrap it around my waist, tightening it enough to ensure if I bleed again, it will help stop it.

Unhooking the dress, I slip it over my head, wincing as the stretching of my muscles causes the scars to pull. My hair is slightly damp, but I use my fingers to comb through it before letting it hang naturally. I have no clue what the time is and no way of telling it. All electronics and weapons I had on me were confiscated. The one thing I have left is my lightning, but I will only use it if I need to. Perhaps this meeting will gain me another powerful ally.

A yawn escapes me, and I eye the bed of furs. "A small nap couldn't hurt."

I nestled down between the furs, snuggling into the warmth.

"You know the real reason you find yourself pinned beneath me again?" His fingers tease as they move up my inner thigh, his lips nip at my ear, making my pussy throb. I can't help

but push back against him. I feel his erection digging into my ass. The only thing separating us are the clothes on our bodies. "I can smell your arousal." He purrs while teasing those fingertips up and down my inner thigh.

I reach behind me, gripping the back of his neck while my other hand grips the furs beneath me. "Please..." I beg breathlessly, desperately wanting him to touch me again. To make me feel the way I did the first time we were together.

"Hmm. I love hearing you beg." He growls in my ear before running his tongue down the length of my neck. A moan escapes me as I push back against him. "What do you want, Sunshine?"

Sunshine? Alexxander has never called me that, only...

My eyes snap open as I wipe the sweat from my brow before tossing the covers from my body and pushing to my feet. I can feel the evidence of my sex dream dripping down my legs. Racing to the bathroom, I quickly grab the cloth and clean myself up before splashing my face with water. I look into the mirror, but don't recognize the woman staring back at me. "We can't go there. Not again, and especially not with him."

I will not think of either of them. Besides, neither of them showed up to rescue me. Not that I need anyone, no less a man, to save me. After exiting the bathroom, I go to the door and tug it open. It opens without effort. A cool breeze hits me, carrying with it the smell of cooking meat. My stomach growls as I grip my injured side while peeking out into the hall. When I see it's empty, I go left, because there is nothing but a wall to the right. It could be a trick or a trap, but I'm not armed, and Nefretiri stated I was her guest.

I walk down the hall and try to remember which way

C.M. HANO

Emanuel brought me when we came inside. The house isn't large, so it shouldn't be too difficult to make it out. Right? At the end of the corridor, I turn right, and then left, and repeat the same maneuver five times before I make it into an open space. In front of me is nothing but a blank wall. "Fuck! How hard is it to get out of a tiny hut?"

"Easy." Emanuel's sly voice comes from behind me, and I whip around to face him. His mask is gone. I wouldn't call him ugly, but I wouldn't say he isn't the most good-looking man I've ever laid eyes upon. He walks up to me, his bare chest peeking out between an open, long-sleeved vest. I keep my eyes locked on his as the scent of pine and smoke comes from him. "If you know where you are going." He holds out his elbow for me to take. I eye it, but cock a brow, showing him I don't blindly trust someone who just kidnapped me.

He chuckles. The sound deep and rumbling in his chest as his smile widens. No missing or decaying teeth. No hint of bad breath. "If you can trust a shifter, you can trust me."

"Doubtful." I state, stepping away from him.

"If we wanted you dead, Your Highness," he pauses, stepping up to me once more, reaching out to tuck a curl behind my ear. My hand snaps out on its own and I grip his wrist. Hard. I can feel my power surfacing as I bare my teeth at him.

"Don't. Touch. Me." He eyes me curiously before retracting his hand.

"You've got a powerful grip. I'd hate to see what you can do in a fight." He compliments me while shaking his wrist out and then rubbing it.

As if I could hurt you.

"Come. Chief doesn't take kindly to tardiness. Especially

19

for the guest of honor."

"Lead the way." I gesture for him to walk. He holds out his elbow once more, but I shake my head. "I will walk beside you, but I will not touch you."

He nods then drops his arm back by his side. We walk in silence as I follow him back through the maze of corridors until we come to a stop at a door. "Wait, this wasn't here before. How?"

Instead of answering my question, he pushes it open and walks through, holding it for me to follow. "If we wanted you to know our secrets, then you'd have been out here an hour ago."

The door closes behind me as I follow Emanuel down the stairs onto the cobblestone path. The streets are empty, the air quiet, the only light comes from the full moon and a distant glow from a fire atop a hill in the distance.

As we move closer, I can hear music growing, drumming in my ears along with the chanting of voices. Some words I recognize from the ancient texts in the library. Others... let's just say I didn't study languages.

"deos lauda, Ne timeas eos, deos audi, Noli obmutescere, Di libera, Noli recipere."

"What does it mean?" I whisper in Emanuel's ear as we stop just outside the circle.

"It's a prayer. Come, sit. Chief is waiting for you." I follow him around the group, listening to their songs before taking a seat on a black pillow next to Nefretiri. Her dress... outfit barely covers her body. It's made of a bra and panties, with sheer black lace covering the rest of her body. Her black hair is braided into a crown at the back of her head and her markings are painted gold. She looks just as regal as any royal in Constellina.

The music stops, and she opens her arms wide, earning the attention of every one of her subjects before speaking. "Tonight, we honor Princess Gwenyfer of the Sagittarian Court."

I wave, but a piece of meat is shoved in my face by a servant I didn't see. Looking around, I catch a glimpse of Emanuel, who gestures for me to bite it. I do, and the entire group shouts with glee before more plates are brought out. The meat tastes nothing like pig or cow, but it's tangy and has a gamey flavor. A servant hands me a cup filled with purple liquid. I raise the cup to my lips, but rather than taking a sip, I sniff it instead.

"It isn't poisoned." Nefretiri drawls as she takes the cup, locking eyes with me as she takes a sip. I watch as her tongue darts out to lick the juices from her lips. Gods, that's hot. She holds the chalice up to my lips, and I take a tentative swallow. "You like?"

"Yes." I choke out.

"It's fae wine. Homemade right here in Nezar by my farmers."

"Fae? Do you mean faeries? You still exist?" The last I heard about them was that they are the ancestors of the dragon shifters.

"Of course we do. How do you think the world has remained alive for so long?"

"You take care of it. How? I mean, I thought the shifters were the only magical beings left aside from the gods." She takes a piece of bread, dips it into a brown gravy, then offers it to me. I bite into it and almost moan at the burst of flavor. The dough, salt, and butter are in perfect harmony with the meaty gravy.

She smiles at me. "If I told just anyone of our existence, then we wouldn't be here."

"True. I imagine King Outher would try to steal your magic or kill you all."

"You're very morbid."

"Yes, well, when you've been around death and threats for as long as I have, you'd be just as comfortable talking about it as me." She places a hand over mine. It's so unfamiliar that I flinch.

"Tell me what you know of the dragon king, and why you were heading to his palace with his sons?" How? She was watching us, of course. "I know everything that happens in my forest."

I sigh. "It's a long story, and as you said, if I told you everything, then I would be worm food."

Her eyes narrow, "Convince me that humans are redeemable."

"How?" I ask and she shrugs while taking another sip of wine.

"Agree to be tested. If you prove yourself, then I will be your ally." She looks out at her people engaged in their conversations, drinking, and eating. Some appear to be drunk as lips and hands connect and clothes are slowly stripped. I look away as Emanuel walks over, his vest gone, and he gets on his knees before us.

"Um, perhaps I should leave." I suggest at the same moment his lips slam against Nefretiri's neck, and she opens her legs for him. I try to look anywhere but at them as heat creeps into my cheeks. Though I feel a hollowness in my chest that does nothing but remind me of Alexxander's betrayal. A moan escapes her as Emanuel dips his head beneath the lace and he eats her out right in front of me. I stand as the area turns from feasting on food to a different form of hunger.

"Tomorrow, I expect an answer," Nefretiri states as she moves to straddle Emanuel, who is now completely naked and then they grow as she rides him. I pry my eyes away and start my descent down the hill.

"This is the weirdest night of my life." I swipe a hand down my face as I reach the street that leads back to my little house. Everything is quiet down here. No one is naked or having sex around me. I understand all cultures are different, but I like to keep my sex life private. Not that there isn't anything wrong with what the Nezar people indulge in. They seem peaceful and happy. I have seen nothing or heard anyone threaten another person. It's a delightful change of pace.

I stop at the house as a thought crosses my mind.

Once I'm on the roof, I find a pleasant spot and lay down, looking at the stars to bask in the peace of this place. "It's so quiet."

A few minutes go by and then it registers. "I'm alone. Unguarded."

I jump from the roof, using the momentum from the landing to take off into a sprint down to where we entered. But once I reach the forest wall, I feel around for the false door. "Where the fuck is it?" I whisper-yell.

I scan the area, glancing over my shoulder but see nothing except the distant glow from atop the hill. *Calm down, we're alone and we have time.*

A branch cracks and I still. Getting into a fighting stance, I try to see through the darkness. Ready to fight for my freedom. Then, I feel it. Not wanting to get captured again,

I swing out with my right fist and connect with a jaw and then kick my foot out and hit the person square in their groin. "Fuck, Sunshine."

"Arthur?" I reach out, kneeling in front of him before wrapping my arms around his neck while inhaling his familiar moonflower and ash scent. "Shit. How did you get in here?"

"Not here. Come with me." I interlock my fingers with his, my stomach fluttering at the feel of his skin touching mine. He pulls me down the border into a small maintenance shed. The door closes, and I can't see anything. "I can't light a flame or else we could be seen, but this is secure for now."

"Arthur, how did you find me?" I whisper as I let go of his hand to wrap my arms around myself. My vision adjusts and I can make out the jade color of his eyes.

"I followed you." He answers with a shrug as if it wasn't a big deal that I was taken.

He let them take me. "You mean, you let them take me. You and your brother."

His white smug smirk comes before the purr in his voice, and I can feel the tips of his boots kiss mine as my back hits the wall and his arms lock me in. "Damn, Sunshine. He hurt you so badly you can't even say his name when he isn't around." I feel his fingertips reach out as he tucks a strand of hair behind my ear before trailing the tip down my neck. "Do you want to kill my brother?"

"No," I whisper, swallowing the dryness in my throat.

"Liar." He purrs. "Your pulse is racing. You're either lying or..." His breath kisses my lips and I look at them. Flashes of my dreams make me squirm.

"Or?" I challenge him, trying to maintain some type of control. He leans forward and my lips part as I prepare for him to kiss me. But he whispers in my ear.

"You're feeling guilty, Sunshine. Did you fuck someone else? Let them touch you just so you could get over him?" A bucket of ice water sizzles out any heat I was feeling, and my hand moves as I slap him across the face. Only it didn't land. He catches my wrist and then the other and pins them behind my back.

"Fuck you, Arthur Penddragon. It's none of your or his business who I decide to fuck." He smirks as he inhales my scent. His eyes narrow, his nostrils flaring before he looks deep into my eyes, putting both my wrists into one iron hold in a single hand before his fingers skim down my body. "What are you doing? Stop that and let go of me."

I realize what he's looking for the moment his hand lands on it and I hiss in pain, my forehead landing on his chest. "I'm only going to ask this once." I lift my head and he grips my chin, letting go of my other hand in the process, and in a voice as cold as death he speaks, "Who the fuck did this to you?"

CHAPTER THREE

Gwen

I am speechless. Stunned in place while the heat from his glare bores into me.

He doesn't care about me. He just wants to use my power and position to kill his father.

"No one. I did it to myself." I push him away as I limp towards what I think is a bench seat, not wanting to look at him while I lie. It's none of his business, anyway.

"Bullshit, Gwenyfer." He growls. "You can lie to everyone else, but you can't lie to me."

I spin on my heel, my eyes blazing. "You don't know me! And you don't own me! We're using each other for a power move. I'm using you to gain control of my power and to save my friends from Locknite. To take back my throne. And you're using me for... fuck if I know." I close the distance between us and with all the hate I can muster, say "I'm not some damsel in distress who needs a no-magic low life to save her. You and your brother can fuck off for all I care."

His expression goes stoic, but he doesn't move, not until I go to pull the door open. He pushes it closed, locking it as he cages me in his arms again. I can feel his chest pressing against my back, his lips a breath away from my neck. "If you want me to leave, then so be it. But I can't promise you I won't stop watching over you. You're–"

"Shut up." I interrupt. "I don't need a guardian angel. Leave me alone. It was a mistake trusting you and Alexxander."

"Tell me something, Gwenyfer. If you hate both of us, if you hate me, then why can't you turn around and look at me when you dismiss me?" I don't speak. Don't move because if I tell him the truth about how I've been dreaming about him, how my mind is consumed by thoughts of him and not Alexxander, it would make me a traitor. "At least be woman enough to look me in the eye and lie."

I take a shuddering breath and turn towards him, preparing to do just as he asked. Our eyes lock, and I can't bring myself to dismiss him. Though I'm not ready to address whatever's happening between us.

"I'm here to ally with the Chief. She wants me to agree to a test to prove humans are redeemable and can be trusted. I have until morning to make my choice. If you want to stay, you should know they don't like you but, I will ask her to spare your life on account that you're my bodyguard and nothing more." I explain, somehow managing to keep my voice firm.

"Your bodyguard? That's all I am to you?" He asks. Was that a flash of pain in his eyes? What does he expect? Me to call him a friend? He's an acquaintance. Sure, I lust for him, but I don't know him well enough to consider wanting more. I won't make that mistake again.

I tilt my chin up, "Yes."

"If I agree to play my part of bodyguard, then you have to accept everything that means." I raise a brow, but don't question it. I nod, but he smirks. "That's not how shifters make—"

He takes me by surprise as his lips press against mine. I stand completely still, conflicted with the urge to push him away and pull him closer. His arms close around me, and I almost forget everything else. Almost. Before it can go any further, I break away. "I have enough cuts on my body. I didn't want another one." It was a peck on his lips, nothing like I imagined an actual kiss between us would feel.

"You call that a kiss?" He asks. I don't have time to answer and soon his mouth is against mine, his tongue penetrating my lips as his hands move my ass and he lifts me in the air. I wrap my legs around his waist, my back hitting the wall as his mouth expertly claims mine. My pussy throbs and I can feel my nipples harder against the fabric of my dress. This is the kiss I've been imagining happening between us.

There is more than just longing, something sparks inside of my stomach, and I can feel the humming of magic. I break away from Arthur, his lips landing on my neck as I feel his erection pressing against me. A moan escapes my lips and then I look down at my hands. "Arthur." It comes out breathy. "Wait. Stop."

"Damn it, Sunshine." He backs away from me as his eyes land on the pink lightning dancing along my fingers. "Now we know what lust will cause you to do."

The pink fades away as his word registers. 'Lust'. Right, because that's all a man like him would ever see me as. Another body to claim. I pull up an invisible wall between us and calm myself. "So we have an agreement."

"Yeah. I'll be your fake bodyguard."

Alexxander crosses my mind for a second and I hope I don't regret asking this next question. "Where is your brother?"

"Don't know. Don't care. Show me to your room. I need to look at your wounds and you need rest before these tests." Arthur keeps talking but I zone him out as I lead him to where I've been staying.

He didn't come for me, again.

He let them take me, again.

He didn't fight for me, again.

He doesn't deserve me.

Alexxander Penddragon never was, nor will he ever be my Fated Mate.

Arthur

Princess Gwenyfer will be the death of me. Literally.

There isn't anything I wouldn't do to protect her. She didn't have to ask me to make a deal to pretend to guard her. I'd do it willingly. I watch her sleep soundly after I cleaned and checked her wounds, nearly losing my self-control and killing every fucking living being in the place for hurting her. Even if they're superficial. Especially after that kiss.

What was that all about? It was unexpected, and I'd only been teasing her to get underneath Alex's skin. But now that he is... well, doing whatever, I should stop and focus on the primary goal: killing my father, destroying my brother, and the other part that little miss Sunshine will never learn about. It doesn't concern her, nor do I need her help with it. Getting my wings back is something she wouldn't be able to help me with anyway.

I can't fuck around with her, she'll be my undoing.

"No! Stop! You lied to me. You're hurting me. Alexxander, please stop!" I race over to her, pulling her into my arms to soothe her just like at the inn.

"What the fuck did my brother do to you?" I'm not sure I want to know, but whatever it is, she has nightmares about it. I want to kill him for making her feel afraid. Ashamed and guarded. I saw what she did after I kissed her. A wall formed fast between us, and if I was a good man, one that didn't like a challenge, I would keep it that way. But I'm not. She was claimed by my brother, and I toyed with her because of him, but now? I want to break every brick she placed between us until she is mine. Not just in body, but mind and soul.

"Alex?" I look down to see her eyes are half open. "You came back. I love you." She's dreaming. I know she is, but, fuck if that doesn't wound me. I know we're twins but I thought she could tell the difference between us. A sob breaks from her throat as tears trickle down her cheeks while she tosses and turns. I tighten my hold on her, trying to soothe her again. "I don't love you anymore. I kissed him. I kissed him. I kiss…"

"It's okay, Sunshine. You're safe. He'll never hurt you or touch you again. I'll make sure of that because now that I've gotten a small taste, I'll be damned if I let you get away."

My brother is a fool, but I'm not.

Gwenyfer will be mine and no one will prevent me from

getting what's mine ever again.

Alexxander

I snap awake at the sound of a squirrel nibbling an acorn nearby.

The fire is out and Arthur's nowhere to be seen.

I stand, brushing the dirt off my pants as I look for him. Reaching into my pocket, I pull out the phone I snagged while I went back to Kalice City to clean up. I look at the local news circulating to see a press conference that the prince of Scorpion Court just attended. Clicking on it, I watch as he informs reporters of what the humans are calling: *War of Courts.*

"Prince Lance, have you heard from any of the other royal courts?" A news reporter asks.

"I have, but for their safety and the security of information, I will not tell you when or who."

"Are they gathering the armies? Has there been a draft to recruit soldiers?" Another reporter quickly added.

"The Constellina draft has been activated. Those who are eligible to serve are already at a secure training location. Have no fear, citizens, we will win this war." The prince answers with confidence. "Are there any more questions?"

"What a dick." Arthur startles me.

"Have you met him?" I ask, looking up from the screen. He shakes his head. "Where did you go?"

"To see our little princess." He smirks. "Before you go all hot headed on me, yes, I was able to get past their magic, no, I won't tell you how, and yes, she's in love with me."

He holds his hands up in surrender at my answering snarl. "You're such an asshole. If you can figure out how to get over, so can I."

His hand lands on my chest, halting me. "Remember what I told you about space?"

"What the fuck am I supposed to do? Sit out here with my thumb up my ass while I wait for her to forgive me.?" I growl, raking my hands through my hair.

Arthur laughs at that, "No. Why not make yourself useful and start gathering allies? Once we get out of the little fae town, Sunshine will be so delighted that you did that just for her."

He has a point, although he said it in a way that makes me want to knock his teeth out. "Fine. I'll meet you back here. Just…keep her safe."

I don't wait for him to agree as I spread my wings and take flight. Making my way to the Scorpion Court will take an hour or so, but that gives me time to think about strategy. How can I convince these humans I'm on their side? Would they listen to me? The time to find out came a lot sooner than I anticipated as I pull up the world map on my phone to a new press release announcing the prince has moved to one of his many warships, sailing to an undisclosed location.

I stop mid-air, noticing I'm directly over the sea.

Gliding down, I spot his large fleet of matching ships.

Pointing out which one could be his was going to be a lot more difficult than just finding the obvious one. I fly lower, using the sails to hide as I go from one to next, looking for anything out of place or different from the rest. After about ten ships and thirty more minutes, I notice a young man that resembles the prince. He could be a decoy, but I have to risk it.

Without warning, I land on the deck with a loud bang,

gaining their attention. The captain pushes the prince behind him while drawing his curved sword.

"Prince Lance, I'm not here to fight. I Just want to speak with you." I announce, holding my hands up to show I mean no harm.

"We don't negotiate with shifters." The Captain shouts.

"I believe I was talking to the man behind you. With all due respect, this is on behalf of Princess Gwenyfer. She needs your help, and I'm here to discuss terms of an alliance with you." I should be an ambassador instead of a mafia don.

"Let him speak." I expected the voice to come from behind the captain, but instead, it came from behind me. "I'm the prince. We'll discuss these terms in my quarters."

I follow him down a flight of stairs into his chambers. A large room with a four-poster bed, desk, table and chairs, and my personal favorite; a liquor cabinet.

"Would you like a drink?" He asks.

"No, as I said, just here on business."

"Then take a seat, Shifter Prince." He gestures to the table, and I pull out a chair. "So you're the one?" I raise a brow as he turns to face me, a cup of whiskey in hand. "The one who ran off with the princess, or was it kidnapped?" He sips. I open my mouth to speak, but he continues. "No, my favorite is the one where they say she fell in love, eloped, and ran off into the sunset as happy as can be in the arms of her shifter prince."

"None of those are true, as you can see, I'm here because I don't wish to see King Outher take over the realm. We need your armies as well as you need hers. Each court can contribute to the ranks and march against my father. Princess Gwenyfer just needs a meeting spot, and she will be there with her army at her back." I explain.

"Right. Well, I'll look to it. I will send word once we have a location, time, and meeting place. Just ensure the princess understands what this means." I raise a brow at that. "That even if she did fall for a shifter, she's still a human, and a human is who will rule by her side when this is all over."

"And let me guess, you intend that to be you?" This arrogant, pompous ass thinks he has a shot with my princess? She wouldn't touch him with a ten-foot pole.

"Yes, we're a perfect match. She's a princess, I'm a prince. Clearly both of us are attractive, our children will be blessed." I let him enjoy his delusion for a minute before standing as I pull out my phone. We exchange numbers before I leave, ready to be rid of Prince Lance's fantasy about someday marrying my mate.

I decide to make a quick detour in Kalice City for a supply run. Clothes, food, and to adorn some more sensible clothing for camping in the forest. A tent and bedroll, just enough for me since Arthur managed to weasel his way inside. The bastard. When I land, it's dark and I take the time to set up my temporary home, heating up a can of potato soup for my dinner.

Memories of my time with Gwen filter through my head, just as they do every night. The last image is of her face before her eyes shone with hate.

CHAPTER FOUR

Gwen

I'm a warrior standing in front of a mirror, wearing another gown. Only this one has red layered skirts tiered around a long-sleeved white gown. I pull my hair up into a high ponytail, taking one last glance at my reflection before leaving the room. I find Arthur standing at the door, speaking to someone through the crack. His voice is too low for me to hear, and I don't think they realize I am in here because when I clear my throat, he doesn't glance back. The door closes as he turns to look at me. His eyes rove over me from head to toe, and I swear I hear the mocking before it leaves his lips.

"Don't say it," I say before I head over to the door.

He steps into my path. "Good morning, Sunshine. I believe it's time to escort you to the Chief's chambers. Or whatever."

"Who were you talking to?" I narrow my eyes at him.

"Doesn't matter. What does is that we need to leave now before she goes to get the cavalry. You haven't declared me yours yet. So unless you want to be responsible for someone dying, then I suggest we get this over with." He raises a brow in challenge.

As we make our way down the hall, I try to remember the way Emanuel took us, but I doubt myself. Arthur remains silent until the fifth wrong turn.

"Are we lost?"

"Yes. I mean, I thought I could get us out of here. I Thought I could remember the way but... ugh!" I am exhausted and flustered.

"Calm down."

"We're lost, and if I don't tell Nefretiri I will do this test, then we're dead." My breathing becomes heavy. My fists clench, and I feel my power pushing forward.

"Gwenyfer, look at me," Arthur commands, but I can't. I know that if I do, I will lose control. He reaches for me, but I step back. "Alright, fine." He throws his hands up in exasperation.

I close my eyes and breathe, regaining control as I feel my power retreat. When I look at Arthur's face, his typical stoic expression is in place once again. "See? I told you; I've got this."

"Whatever you say, Sunshine." He shrugs. I hear something in his tone. Pain? Rejection? It couldn't be.

"Well, this is interesting." Fuck.

"Emanuel, I can explain."

"Not to me. Chief is waiting." We follow him through the door, and I blink twice.

"I checked this wall three times," I state while catching up to Emanuel.

"Don't worry, Your Highness, if all goes the way the Chief wants it, you will know your way around Nezar soon." He answers and my gut clenches. What does he mean by that? I look over my shoulder, concerned with Arthur's unusual silence. He looks just like the guards back at the palace always did. That's good. It means there will be no more sex dreams, passionate kisses, or teasing touches. It's the right thing to do. But why does it feel so wrong?

We walk into the lobby, only this time, it's filled with people. I spot Nefretiri front and center, sitting on a pillow atop a raised platform. She's dressed in the same fashion as last night. "Princess Gwenyfer, I see you've brought one heir into my home. Now, give me one reason why I shouldn't kill him on site?"

"He's not an heir anymore." The room reverberates with an awe sound.

"Has he abdicated his throne? Abandoned his family and kingdom?" She asks.. I catch a glimpse of Arthur's jaw tightening in my periphery.

"Not exactly. He's chosen to be my bodyguard." I announce. The tension in the room grows palpable. I look at Nefretiri's eyes narrow in suspicion. *Fuck. I need to come up with something more.* "And…"

"What are you doing, Sunshine?" Arthur hisses in my ear. I can see his hand gripping the hilt of his sword. "Come up with something or else I will."

I freeze.

I can do this. I can speak to another leader to find a diplomatic resolution. I was trained to be a Queen, after all. I'm supposed to be on my way to Locknite, supposed to be saving my friends while gathering the relics gifted by Gods so I can get answers about who and what I am. But this visit might just tip the scales in my favor. If I can form an alliance with Nefretiri and her people, then maybe there's a way we can actually beat King Outher.

It's a long shot, but it's all I have.

Though before I can even get my next words out, Arthur says something disastrous.

"And I'm her fiancé."

"You, her bodyguard, and her fiancé?" Nefretiri questions. I can feel her eyes on me, but I keep my chin tilted up, not wanting her to know that *wasn't* the plan. I guess I have no choice but to run with it now. "Princess Gwenyfer, do you expect me to believe that Arthur Penddragon is to marry you? A human woman from his enemy court?"

"Yes. He and I will be married." The room stays silent, but I continue as I wipe my clammy hands down the back of my skirt. "Arthur Penddragon is to be my husband. My Queen Consort and father of my children. I'm marrying a dragon shifter." The lies sizzle on my tongue.

Nefretiri's eyes narrow. "If that is true, then where is your symbol?" Symbol? She means a ring.

"It's in a safe spot until after the war," Arthur says, and as much as I want to kill him for this, I also want to thank him.

"Right. We will have your wedding here. As soon as I am convinced you can be trusted. Princess Gwenyfer, if you agree to my test, then I will be your ally. Not only will we celebrate our new alliance, but we will also celebrate your marriage." Nefretiri announces with a gleam in her eyes.

"Can I just have one moment with my beloved?" Arthur asks. I almost don't stop myself from exhaling in time.

"Of course. There is an alcove right there. I will give you two minutes"'" Arthur takes my hand tenderly, the way a fiancé might as he leads me to the alcove. Soon, I'm enclosed into a small dark space with Arthur fucking Penddragon, again. Goddess helps me.

"Are you okay, Sunshine?"

I scoff and then punch him in the arm. "Engaged? That was the best you could come up with?"

"Well, you said nothing, and I knew a Chief would never kill the lover of a royal. She seems too honorable for that."

"Well, great, because once I pass these tests, we will be married, and it won't be fake. It will be real and for all eternity."

"Wow." He scoffs, looking at me with anger in his eyes. "You would've rather been dead than married to me? Damn. That hurts."

"Arthur, no. It's just–"

"It's cool, Your Highness. Once you pass those tests before we have to get married, I'll make myself disappear and you'll never have to see me again." The door opens before I can protest, but I see Emanuel standing there with a raised brow. He suspects our lies.

I walk to the center of the room. "I will agree to whatever test you choose, Chief Nefretiri. And I'd be honored to marry Arthur on your land in the presence of a new friend."

Everything and everyone waits on abated breath for her next command. I watch as she stands and closes the distance between us. "Your first trial shall start tomorrow. If you pass, you'll take a couple of days' rest before the next. And if you pass the second one, another week will pass before your final one. By the end of the month, we will see if you have a new ally or a new enemy."

A month? Tori and the people don't have that long.

"I can't stay here for a month." She crosses her arms as she waits for me to explain. "I have friends that are wrongfully imprisoned in Locknite. I was on my way there to free them when Emanuel captured me. If I stay here, by the time I leave, they'll most likely be dead."

"That is very noble of you, Princess Gwenyfer. It says a lot about a leader who would sacrifice her own freedom for her subjects." She sighs. "However, I can't let you leave just yet, but if you pass the first trial tomorrow, I will grant you partial freedom so that you may free your friends from prison. Under supervision, of course. Can you agree to those terms?"

I'm outnumbered here. In order to survive this night, I'll agree to her terms. Once on the outside of these mysterious walls, I can figure a way to escape from whomever she sends with me.

"Yes." I answer without hesitation as I hold out my hand. When she looks at it, I momentarily panic, thinking she'll be like a shifter, wanting blood or a kiss, but she spits in her palm and waits for me to do the same to mine. Gods, this is gross. We slap palms and I almost throw up at the feel of our saliva mixing.

"Princess Gwenyfer and Arthur Penddragon are now the most precious guests. They will need an upgraded house and are to be left alone for the day. Emanuel, you are to be their guide and get them whatever they need. I want her highness to be fully prepared for tomorrow."

"Yes, Chief."

"See you in the morning." With her farewell, Emanuel ushers us out of the house, down the street, and towards the market area. Everyone is busy at work just like they were when I arrived here yesterday. A gust of wind carries various aromas, and I can't help but smile as it warms my soul.

"Don't get too comfortable, Your Highness. We're still in enemy territory here." Arthur warns. My pace slows as I watch him walk ahead. The one-eighty he's done in the last twenty-four hours about us is painful. I once asked him to stop calling me by his chosen nickname, but hearing him address me so formally, feels wrong.

It's good, Gwen. It means there is no possibility of distraction. I tell myself but my inner voice doesn't sound too convinced, and neither am I.

Arthur

I don't trust these faeries.

There's something about them that has my hackles raising and I'm too stupid for my own good to not leave her royal pain in my ass behind. This woman is so damn infuriating that I swear if I didn't want to fuck her, I'd kill her.

"Is this suitable?" Emanuel asks as I look at the two-story building in front of us.

"Are there any mazes in there?" Gwenyfer asks.

"No, Your Highness." He chuckles. "It is a regular house, and you'll find everything you need inside. Now, you are not to leave until I come for you tomorrow morning. If you do, it will break the peace." His tone drops to a serious note, and again, my instincts scream at me to run. But I won't. Not this time. Not ever.

"What about food?" She asks.

"Meals will be provided. I'm sorry to cut this short but you must get inside. I will have to lock the door." He states. I watch as Gwenyfer gives him a thumbs up before taking the stairs two at a time. I step through the door, ensuring he is the only one who can hear me while I keep my eyes on her.

"Look at her. Don't look at me." I can see him staring out of the corner of my eye. My focus goes to him, and I whisper, in a tone as cold as ice. "I will kill anyone who threatens her, and if you think for one second, you're off the hook for hurting her, you're mistaken."

He turns his gaze to me. Golden eyes narrowed with a smirk. "When the Chief figures out you both lied to her about this fake engagement, you won't have to worry about anyone hurting her. You'll both be dead."

He steps away but I grip his arm, my talons piercing his skin as they elongate. "Just a reminder as to why you are secluded in this little forest bubble." My flames dance in my eyes, letting him know just how serious I am. "You will get yours for hurting her. And when you do, everyone will know it was me who did it because I'm not a coward." I retract my hand and pat him on the back. "Good talk."

I make my way into the house, closing the door and moving to lock it, only there is none. A smirk curves my lips at the lock clicking shut by some other force. *These people have no idea what kind of beast they just caged.*

"Arthur?" Gwenyfer calls out for me. I exit the foyer to find a lounge area with nothing in it but a stone fireplace. "Well, there are two bedrooms. I expect you can sleep down here, and I'll take the room upstairs."

"No."

"Excuse me? That wasn't a suggestion."

"I don't take orders from you, Your Highness."

She scoffs, placing her hands on her hips. "As my

bodyguard, I say you do."

I move closer, knowing how my presence affects her, and relish in every second of it. The way her pulse races, knees buckle, breathing hitches I lean in and whisper between us. "I'm your fake bodyguard. I will not take orders from you."

She swallows and I know I could cross that final line with her. Make her mine fully. Claim her body. But I also love to tease because the moment she finally breaks, I'll fuck the memory of my little brother out of her. "Fine. I'll take downstairs and you take upstairs."

"No." I purr as I place my hands on either side of the wall behind her. "We are meant to be married. To act like we're in love. People who are engaged do not sleep in separate bedrooms. Or separate beds."

"I'm not sharing my bed with you."

"Hmm. Are you afraid you won't be able to control yourself?" My chest and hers barely touch as I run the tip of my tongue along her neck. "I bet you want to know how my tongue would feel on your pussy. I imagine how you'll beg for my cock by the time I'm done with you. You'll want no one else. Because you're not my princess, you're my little whore."

A searing pain comes across my face the second her palm connects with it. I can feel the humming of magic she added to the blow. Before I have time to recover, we've switched positions, and she has me pinned by my throat against the wall. Her eyes glow pink while she cuts off my air. "You'll do as you're told. My friends and my people will not die because you think I'll fall into your bed. I'm meant to be the queen of my court." She leans in and whispers in my ear. "And if anyone is going to be called a whore, it's you. Now, get on your knees and beg for my forgiveness."

Fuck! If I wasn't already hard before, now my cock is begging to be inside her. She releases me and I suck in a sharp breath before kneeling at her feet. I feel her hand grip my chin and lift my eyes to meet hers. There are no words exchanged between us, but I know that at this moment, I will do anything she tells me to do.

Instead of letting her maintain control, I loop my fingers into her pants and jerk them down, causing her to gasp. I bury my nose into her underwear, inhaling her scent. My hands trail up her thighs, hooking into her panties as I slowly pull them down. "Tell me you want this, Sunshine." I run my tongue across her soaking pussy, and she opens herself wider for me. Her hand fists my hair as she grinds on me. I keep going, nipping, and biting at her. She tastes just like I suspected she would, and I don't know if I'll ever want to stop after this.

I move my fingers to her pussy and insert two while sucking her clit.

"Arthur," she moans my name, and it sounds better than I imagined it.

"You want more, don't you?" She moans again and I add a third finger, going faster, matching the pace of her hips until she clenches down, and I lap up every ounce of her juices. "Fuck, Sunshine, you taste amazing."

She pulls her clothes back up, grips my chin, swiping a thumb across it then placing it in my mouth. I suck it and her eyes alight with desire. When I'm ready to pounce and truly fuck her, she digs her nails into my skin in warning.

"I don't wish to see you for the rest of the day. Don't disturb me unless it's for food or an emergency. Got it?" She asks and I nod, still too mesmerized by the sheer strength and power she just displayed. I watch as she makes her way up the stairs, my dick painfully straining in my pants.

"You have no idea what you just started, Sunshine."

Inside the bathroom, I turn the shower hot, using the soap to lather up my dick and pump it. Visions of her on her knees, those eyes watering as I hit the back of her throat. "That's right, Sunshine takes my cock." I speak out loud, uncaring if she can hear me. I want her to know what she just fucking did to me. My hand moves faster, and I squeeze, imagining taking her cunt and slamming myself into her with her dark curls wrapped in my fist as I kept a punishing pace.

A new image flashes in my head, one that I wasn't expecting. Gwenyfer on all four, her ass exposed with my tip swirling at her perched entrance ready to take me. I push in and she screams my name. "I'm the alpha here, Sunshine." She's tight and I fuck her ass, hard, fast just as I should when claiming my mate in this way. Before I could realize what I just said, I'm coming in my hand, the weight of my fantasy crashing into me.

"Fuck. No. She can't be."

But then again, what if?

CHAPTER FIVE

Gwen

I take the stairs two at a time, ready to get away from *him*. I don't know what came over me, but it felt empowering and new. Seeing Arthur on his knees before me has my head spinning with an intoxicating power. My panties are soaked, and I need to clean up, but gods I was one second away from letting him fuck me over the couch.

When I make it to the top, I look over the balcony, searching for him but all I can see is the wood floor and stone fireplace. I shrug it off as I walk to the only door up here.

The room is nothing like I expected it to be. A single bed covered in furs sits flush against the back wall and nothing more.. "And this is supposed to be a guest house? Where is the bathroom?" I ask to no one in particular.

I shut the door behind me as I make my way over to the

bed, brushing my fingers over the soft blanket. They're hunting animals in the south. Which means they have ways to travel around the realm without being detected.

My eyes widen with the thought. I make my way back downstairs and bang on Arthur's door. I wait, watching for the turning of the doorknob but nothing happens. Raising my fist once more, I bang and shout, "Arthur! Arthur, open up, I need to talk to you!"

When there is still nothing but silence, I turn the knob, swinging the door open A cloud of steam greets me, forcing me to squint until my eyes land on a naked male body littered with scars. Some small, others look like they'd been made with long, serrated edged blades meant for sawing through bone. The two biggest are right where his shoulder blades end, in the same spot I've seen Alexxander's wings burst from.

I feel my throat dry as I cup my mouth as anger takes over at the thought of who hurt him. My power ignites along my fingers, causing my attention to shift from him to the pink fire zapping between my fingers.

"The shower is in here if you need to use it." Arthur states and I look back at him. This time meeting his face. I don't stop my gaze from traveling down his body, taking steps toward him until my fingers stretch out to trace a scar that runs along the sternum of his chest, down the trail of hair across his navel, and stopping just above his pubic hair. I swallow hard at the erect length of him and retract my hand.

"Don't stop on my account." He smirks.

"I'm sorry." It comes out breathlessly due to my heart thundering in my chest, my emotions swirling inside of me as one tries to take control over the other. "What…who did this…was it your father?"

"Doesn't matter." He says before reaching out to cup my chin, forcing my eyes to meet his. "If you touch me like that again or look at me with hunger in your eyes, I won't be responsible for what happens to you when I lose control."

Was that a dare? Does he want me to push him over the edge? *Get away from him. He is the brother of a man who nearly broke you.* A little voice in my head says I should walk away, treat him like the fake bodyguard he is pretending to be. But his presence fogs my judgment. His scent causes desire to ache between my thighs and my heart to race when I'm around him. I will not lie to myself and say that I am not physically attracted to him, but it's more than that. My body responds like this every time he steps into my line of sight.

"This is dangerous," I whisper. His thumb catches my bottom lip as he leans forward, but I step away from him, nearly making it out of the room before stopping.

I turn my back to him, "We need to become allies with these people. They can travel anywhere and everywhere undetected."

"How do you know that?" He asks.

"Polar bear fur," I answer. "It's on the bed, which means they've traveled to the south, hunted the poor creature, and brought it back without being arrested for poaching a protected animal."

He doesn't respond. I listen for any sound of movement behind me, my pulse jumping as warmth kisses the back of my neck, followed by the scent of moonflower and ash.

His whispered words caress the shell of my ear, "Then I guess you better pass each trial they throw at you and play my pretty little wife when the time comes."

"I won't marry you, Arthur." I crane my neck sideways, giving him access if he wants to take it. My chest rises and falls as my sex throbs with need. "Goodnight, Arthur."

Arthur

She saw and didn't shy away.

I smelled her before she walked through the door and purposely didn't cover up. It wasn't my intention to cause her to lose focus. Even so, it was empowering to see the way she reacted. Her body tensed and her thighs pressed together as her power danced along her fingertips with her desire for me. This means that at the end of this war, she'll either hate me for doing this or love me. I can pray for the latter, but I expect the former because I've already lied to her.

I kept the truth about my brother's absence to myself.

I pull on the clean clothes provided by the Chief; black pants and a long-sleeved shirt before pulling my boots on and walking out into the main area. I look up at her closed door, trepidation flooding my veins as the urge to go to her consumes me.

Running my fingers through my damp hair, I turn towards the front door and turn the knob. It opens, although we were told it would remain locked. Unease twists my stomach, but I fight against it because there is no use in feeling like this. Not when the mission I was given is at risk of failure.

I step out and quietly close the door behind me before scanning the landscape, searching for any sign of guards or villagers. It's dark out, which doesn't comfort me on how time works differently in this little pocket of the world. Walking down the steps and onto the path, I look around once more but see nothing but lit torches on the outside of houses'. It's serene, but too much for my comfort.

Until a deep smooth voice comes from my right, "Scouting for assassins?"

My talons elongate as I turn towards the owner of that voice. "You said the door would be locked but…" I gesture to my obvious presence outside of the house. My dragon's eye takes over as I see his own eyes glow with mischief as a smile spreads across his face.

"Your princess is safe; you, however, are not." He warns.

I chuckle, showing him I'm not afraid of a threat. "Your Chief gave us her word. If she can't keep it, then I will advise my princess not to go into an alliance with someone who has no honor."

"Watch your tongue, dragon." Emanuel snarls. "Chief will hold up her end of the deal as long as your princess does. She is not the one who is threatening to kill you." He moves closer, dust kicking up as he keeps a sword's distance away.

His voice drops to a hushed whisper. "There are those who remember the day your family destroyed our lands. Dragon's burned our cities and ran us out of our homes all because they wanted to be the top shifter."

"I know the history of my people, Faerie." I snarl. "But your people are not all that innocent, either. And if you think they are then you're as naïve as your Chief, believing my father doesn't have spies within this little tree town."

"What do you know?" He grounds out.

I shrug and he growls in response, baring his sharpened canines as I search my memories to find what kind of Fae this man is.

"Tell me what your Chief's intentions are with my princess, and I might oblige your request." I reason. Whether it will be a verbal or physical attack, doesn't matter, because I'm ready for it. A cool breeze blows past us, shaking the limbs of the trees as the scent of rain permeates the air around me. If this Fae is the kind I believe him to be, he will not stay out long. To add to my confirmation, I sniff the air, "It smells like rain."

He snarls and sniffs a few times before he retreats into the shadows without another word spoken between us. When the first droplet hits my cheek, I turn to my left and walk toward the exit. He'll want an update on her condition and the weaknesses of this place. I didn't lie to Gwenyfer when I told her I didn't know where my baby brother was, however, I'm keeping a dangerous and disastrous secret from her. If she knew the truth about me, about the mission I was sent on, she would kill me.

I might just let her, or perhaps fall on my own sword for doing this, but the humans and Alexxander are responsible for what happened to my family. Her parents are the reason that these scars are my permanent reminder of my failure to protect *her*. Gwenyfer is mine in every birthright. The sooner I get past whatever this thing is between us, the clearer my vision will become.

When I make it to the faux door, I reach my hand through and push on it until I can squeeze through the crack. My shoulders are broad, and the gap is tight, pressing into my skin but I can handle it. I learned how to deal with pain a long time ago. Once on the other side, I run.

CHAPTER SIX

Gwen

"I do hope your quarters are to your liking," Nefretiri smiles as we walk side by side down the center path of her village. I didn't sleep last night as thoughts about Arthur consumed me. Questions that need answering, though ones I don't want to ask in fear of the consequences. I didn't see him this morning when I went to bathe. He was probably off wandering about the village for food, but then when I tried to leave, the door was locked. Emanuel had to let me out.

"Yes. They are lovely." I answer with a half-smile.

"Where is your fiancé?" She asks.

I don't know. It's what I want to say, but I decide that to further protect the fool, to come up with something more convincing. "I believe he went for his morning exercise."

She nods as we continue to make our way down the path

towards the large building I met her in. The guards open the doors for us and I blink twice, unsure if what I'm seeing is real or a dream. At the center, a vast feast is laid out on ivory linens that drapes over three long tables.

Gold plated serving dishes and chalices have been laid out symmetrically along the table at each place setting. My mouth waters at the delicious scent of bacon and spiced sausages.

"Are you hosting a party, Chief?" I ask as I follow her to the head of the table.

"Yes. I have invited a few companions of mine to come watch you during your trials." She states as she takes the seat pulled out for her, the golden bangles along her wrist dangling with the movement. The Chief dressed in her usual attire of golden laced clothes that expose the majority of her body. I am dressed in the blue gown she gifted to me with leggings and my boots underneath. While I had pulled my hair up this morning, hers is pinned back with golden clips and braids. She looks like a goddess.

"May I ask who you have requested to join us?" My stomach churns, unsure of who this woman knows and if they are my enemy.

The doors open before she can answer, and a flood of people march in.

I recognize each and every one of them, all dressed in their respective court colors, brooches pinned to their clothes to mark who they are. My eyes land on the man who ordered my assassination. My power surfaces as I see red.

"Your Highness, are you okay?" Nefretiri's question doesn't break my concentration.

Control your emotions, Gwenyfer. Arthur's voice comes from inside of my head. *If you lose control now, you will be dead and then who will be left to kill my father?*

He sounds so close. His presence overshadows my mind, but I listen to him because the time for vengeance is not now. Not when I don't have enough evidence to justify the traitor prince's execution.

"Princess Gwenyfer?" Nefretiri presses as she wraps her cool hand around my own. She jerks back, a slight hiss escaping her teeth as she stares at me with accusation shining in her eyes.

My heart launches into a gallop. That could be classed as assaulting a ruler. She could have me executed for that. "I'm so sorry! Are you okay?" Nefretiri rubs at the red mark on her palm, though it quickly heals in a matter of seconds.

She dismisses my apology, "I'm fine. Is something wrong?" She questions, concern, whether feigned or real, coating her features.

"No. Thank you." I force a tight smile.

She gives me a weary look but brings her attention towards our new company, the heirs of each court within the realm except Tori and —

"Princess Gwenyfer, how delighted we are to see you safe." A feminine, very familiar voice has my heart drumming in my chest. When I turn to look at its owner, I nearly jump out of my seat and run to her.

"Princess Diliha, as am I." Her brown eyes bore into mine, a silent plea to remain quiet until we can speak in private.

"Welcome, rulers of Constellina, I'm pleased to see all of you made it here in a safe and timely manner. The divide between humans and Fae has gone on long enough. That is why I proposed a trial so that one of the human monarchs can prove to me that your kind can be trusted. Princess Gwenyfer of the Sagittarian Court has volunteered to represent you all. If anyone wishes to contest this, please speak now." The room falls silent except for our breathing and I look around at the strange faces in this room, uncertain if any of them will try to replace me, but certain I don't want them to.

When my gaze finally lands on my former fiancé, he smirks and opens his mouth to speak, but I interrupt. "Chief Nefretiri, might I add that if anyone wishes to contest me, that they fight for the right to take my place?"

I give Maurice the same smug smile and he winks at me before adding. "I will fight the princess. After all, it should be a true heir that fights for us humans. Not someone who spread her legs for the enemy."

I'm quick to my feet this time, only I don't get the chance to silence him as a flash of black comes from my right side and Maurice is lifted into the air with Arthur's talons digging into his throat and growling. "Insulting the princess will be the last thing you say."

"Your Highness, I must insist that you call off your guard!" Nefretiri barks, but I walk over to the two of them, looking into Maurice's eyes before placing a hand on Arthur's shoulder. His eyes meet mine and that's when I know who I'm looking at. I inhale his scent just to be sure, and when the smell of ash and spice hits me, I step away.

"Let him go." I order. "And then you can leave."

They both look at me with raised brows, but he lets the human prince fall to the floor with a thud, his spluttering not loud enough to drown out the thumping pulse in my ears.

"Gwen–"

"Go away, Alexxander, before you screw this up for me, too." I dismiss him, turning my back to take my seat once more.

"Does the prince need a healing remedy?" Nefretiri asks. I don't look, knowing that either a servant or whomever he brought with him was seeing to his wounds.

"No, Chief. They are superficial at best." A man states.

"Good. Now, Prince Maurice, are you contesting Princess Gwenyfer's right to fight for the realm of humans?" She slides her eyes to the prince.

"Yes." His voice is hoarse, but not enough to hide his anger. "That woman bedded our enemy. She is the wrong person to represent humans."

Nefretiri looks at me, "Do you agree?"

I tilt my chin up in defiance, "I will fight him, Chief."

"Then so be it. Tomorrow, we will have a duel to determine who will represent the humans in the trials. Everyone, please eat and enjoy." She announces while gesturing to the food. I look at it, but bile rises in my throat.

Although he is an ass, Maurice is correct about one thing, I did bring the enemy into my bed. A good ruler wouldn't do that. She'd be smarter.

"Princess, may I have a word with you?" Alexxander's voice whispers in my ear, but I continue to ignore him as I Pick up my chalice and sip on the sweet wine. "Now. I'm not asking."

He firmly grips my forearm and forces me to my feet, dragging me across the room to the far corner. "Have you lost your senses? I told you to leave." I whisper-yell.

"I told you I wasn't giving up on us." He argues.

"We're not mates. Don't you see that?" I demand, desperation coating my tone.

"Just because we aren't fated doesn't mean we shouldn't be

together." He protests as he reaches for me, but instinctively, I step away.

"I can't."

"Why? I told you that I was lying to you that day in the courtroom. I did it to save your life." He's pleading for me to believe him.

"I know." My gaze drops a touch.

"Then why don't you welcome me back into your heart?"

"Because there is no room for you anymore." It spews out before I can stop it and he flinches, narrowing his eyes.

"You have feelings for him, don't you?" There is an accusation underlying that question, but I remain silent. "He will betray you. My brother is not a good man. He's selfish and cunning. Everything he does and says only benefits him." I keep my gaze to the floor, refusing to look him in the eye. "Fuck, Gwenyfer, at least look me in the eye and tell me the truth."

I snap my eyes to meet his and give him what he wants. "I don't love you anymore, Alexxander. There is no room in my life for you because the only thing I have time for is to train for this war. There is nothing going on between Arthur and me. Nor will there ever be because as you said, he's a selfish bastard, but he came for me, and you didn't."

"I'm here now."

"It's not enough. I need to get back and eat so I have energy for tomorrow." I turn to leave but he grabs me again, I bite the inside of my cheek to hide the pain before looking at him. "You have to let me go."

We stare at each other for a long moment. I can see he understands what I mean and when he nods, releasing my arm, I feel a weight lift off my chest.

"Goodbye, Gwenyfer." That was the last thing he said to me before disappearing into the shadows.

Alexxander

There was an unfamiliar look in her eyes. Nothing like the way they used to brighten when she saw me. Her scent was different, her demeanor, she smelled like *him*. It made me sick to my stomach thinking about why that was. She wouldn't fuck him or let him touch her. except maybe to spite me.

I made my way to my meeting place with the man in question, right outside the village, to find him perched against a tree trunk with a long weed in his mouth. He doesn't move because he knows it's me. It's insulting knowing he doesn't see me as a threat. But it is also his weakness.

"Let me guess, she tried to stab you and then let you go?" His snarky comment does nothing to ease the figurative knife she just gutted me with.

"It's no business of yours, but I do believe that her feelings don't matter. We have a mission, and I don't intend to see what will happen if either of us fail." I kick his boot. "Get up. He's waiting for us."

CHAPTER SEVEN

Gwen

Where is Arthur?

The bastard has been gone since this morning, and I've no clue where he could have gone to, nor how he would be able to leave unnoticed. There are guards everywhere I go. I know it's partly due to me being tethered to Nefretiri, but also because I am seen as a threat. The Nezar don't like humans. That's made obvious by the disgusted looks on their faces whenever one of us passes by.

Even more so since the rest of the realm's monarchs arrived. The event is still on my mind as I follow Nefretiri down a narrow path, leading to another large building. We were all dismissed after breakfast, everyone except for myself because she wanted to show me something.

I was waiting for her to ask about the confrontation in the

hall, but she seemed to understand that there was nothing to discuss. I'm secretly grateful for her lack of interest in me and the men that show up in my life.

We step up a small wooden platform connected to a deck that leads into the two-story building. I inhale the scent of metal and oil before I set my eyes on a few people tinkering away at armor and weapons of varying styles. The workers stop and immediately stand at attention to greet their leader.

"At ease," she says in a smooth tone. "If you're going to fight, I believe you need a weapon." I continue following her further into the main floor, passing over a threshold into a room lined with more swords and daggers. It's quiet in this room. The noise of sharpening stones and humming left outside.

Three walls encompass the small room, each lined with hooks holding weapons of fine work and skill. My fingers itch to run along the hilt, to figure out if it was made from cowhide or deerskin, to hold them and feel for the balance of each before picking out which one perfectly fits my grip and skill.

"They're all beautiful," I whisper.

"Yes. Our blacksmiths are expert craftsmen. I will leave you to choose but once you do, there is no taking it back. So, I'd advise you to choose wisely, but I'm sure you already know that." She winks a playful eye at me before exiting the room and my heart thrums with excitement.

Two beautiful daggers catch my eye in the far back corner. The hilts are simple, wrapped in a fine leather grip. Each blade looks dull, but if I were to touch it, I'm sure it would draw blood.

"Find something you like?" The Blacksmith asks.

"Yes. I'd like to choose these two daggers." He pulls them

off the hook, holds them by the hilt so the sharpened end is pointed to the floor, and offers them to me. I take them and find them perfectly balanced in each hand. Nothing like the ones I was used to carrying around back at home.

"You'll need these as well." He hands me two thigh holsters. After I ensure they're secured in place, I sheath my new daggers. "Good luck tomorrow, Princess."

"Thank you." I exit the small shop and bump into Arthur. "Where have you been?"

He pulls me aside, out of the way of passing guards. "I was taking care of some business."

"What does that mean? You know what, never mind. I don't want to know. I've got more important things to worry about." I push past him, making my way back to our assigned house. I'd love to explore this place more but since the arrival of the other royal dignitaries, the alliance is on thin ice.

"Gwen." I hear Diliha whisper-yell my name. I look around trying to spot her. "Over here. Behind the little hut." I turn my hide side to side trying to locate her. "To your right. Behind the large tree."

I finally see a small ombre glove waving at me through the sea of green leaves.

She pulls in for a hug as soon as I step behind the trunk.

"Where have you been? What happened to you?" I ask. She pulls away from me, tears welling in her eyes. They must be for Tori.

"It was terrible. We were almost to Tori's palace when we were ambushed by these large shifters. Tori and I ran for the safe room, but she fell and twisted her ankle. You know how clumsy she can be. I tried to carry her, but she pushed me off and started limping the other direction, yelling at me to run and find you." She sighs, wiping the falling tears from her cheeks. "She was captured, and they got their hands on the Frozen Star. I only managed to escape by using the secret tunnels like we did when we were kids."

"We'll get her back, D. I promise." I assure her.

"I know we will." She gives me a faint smile. By the expression on her face, I feel as though there is more to this story than she is telling me. "Don't look at me like that, Gwen."

"I wouldn't if I knew you were telling me everything. What are you so afraid to say?" She looks down at her boots, shuffling her feet before answering.

"They weren't all shifters. Some were humans but then they weren't." She pauses. I give her the time to gather her thoughts so she can continue. I know what she is talking about. Alexxander mentioned something about his father using the Golden Star to give human's shifter abilities. "Some of their faces were made of scales–like a dragon. Others had claws instead of hands. They all just looked–"

"Mutated." I finished for her. She nodded. "Outher's using the relics to create these monsters for his army. He's found a way across the Wall of Illusions. Either with the help of the other courts or by other means."

"What are we going to do? Normal humans don't stand a chance against an army like that." She cries.

"I don't want you to worry about that. Tomorrow, I'll secure my spot to compete in the three trials and when I beat those, we'll have a new alliance with one of the most powerful forces to ever exist." She looks at me with admiration in her eyes. "These fae have magic unlike any I've ever seen. With their help, we'll be evenly matched against Outher's army."

"What about Tori? Do you know where she is?"

"Yes. She's in Locknite, but I plan to break her out."

She shakes her head. "You can't. Anyone who goes in never gets out."

I laugh. "Except for me."

"What?"

"After we met in Pittaken Village, I was captured by Alexxander's sister Morgan who brought me to the palace in Dracane Kingdom. Outher had me transported to Locknite, and I was there for a little over a week before I was told I'd have to fight another inmate to the death. I managed to escape." I left out the part about my powers. Diliha doesn't seem to be coping well with the idea that humans can have magic.

"With a little help." We both turn at the sound of Arthur's voice.

"Alexxander?" Diliha gives him a curious look. "No. You're someone else. A twin. Oh my gods, there's another one." She exclaims.

"I'm Arthur, the older, wiser, sexier one." He chimes in.

"He's the annoying one." I add. "He might have helped me but that's beside the point. We have a way into Locknite, but first I need to get out of here."

"And to do that, you have to fight in a duel and go through three trials of unknown danger." Diliha says.

"You make it sound like I'm walking straight up to death's door." I smile.

"We need to get back, Sunshine. Any more time away from our little prison, and Emanuel might become suspicious." Arthur advises.

Diliha and I give each other a brief goodbye. "Be careful

with this one. He looks like he's ready to have you for dinner. And not in the traditional sense."

My relationship with Arthur is nothing but flirtatious passes and unwanted, albeit sexy, dreams. I'm not sure if I can open myself up to getting hurt again. Especially not by the last one's twin brother. I look up at the shifter who is taking a mid-afternoon nap. He looks so relaxed in this setting. He may have the same birthday as Alexxander, every minute I spend with him, I realize just how unalike they are.

"What's on your mind, Sunshine?" He asks.

"Nothing." Everything.

"Then you better have a good reason for creeping on me while I'm sleeping." He pops one eye open to look at me, waiting for me to give him something he'll probably turn into a lude remark. When I don't answer him, he sighs and sits up. His shirt is unbuttoned all the way, giving me the perfect view of his chest.

"Why haven't we tried to escape?" It's something I've been thinking about but just haven't asked about, yet. "I mean, I have magic yet haven't used it once while being here. You haven't encouraged it and I haven't lost control of it. It's almost as if my power is—"

"Dormant." He finishes for me. I meet his gaze, wondering if he knows why that is. "As you told your friend earlier, the fae are a very old, powerful, strong species. They could have a way of suppressing all magic aside from their own. And we haven't tried to escape because your new friend, the Chief, has eyes on you as soon as you walk out of this house."

"Yet, you seem to be able to go wherever you want, whenever you want." I accuse as he leans back against the couch, interlocking his hands behind his head. He doesn't protest and that means, "You've been able to leave here. Haven't you?" He lifts a shoulder in answer. "You were able to get in here without being noticed and that means you know of a way out of here. Tell me."

He shakes his head before saying, "If I tell you, then you'll get yourself hurt trying to leave. Then I'll have to kill whoever touches you and the fae will not be on our side at all." I stand, walk around the coffee table, and lean forward to meet his eye.

"What are you and your brother up to?"

"I have nothing to do with Alexxander. You sent him away, not me."

"Then why was he at the breakfast banquet?"

He moves forward, closing the gap slightly more between us. "Because for some reason, he just can't seem to stay away from you. The one that he believes to be his mate."

"I'm not his mate. The second you both agree with me is the same second we can all move forward."

"Move forward? With who? Got another 'mate' lined up?" We're a breath away from each other and I realize I'm the one who closed the gap this time. My hands are flushed with his thighs, I can feel the seam of his pants rubbing against my thumbs. "Why are you so determined to wipe your memory of him? There must have been something good to come out of all that heartbreak."

The last part was whispered. He has me locked in a trance. Everything about him has me on the edge of a tightrope. One side, the sensible, responsible queen to be, telling me to keep my distance until the war is over. The other, the foolish, reckless woman who just wants to feel something other than pain, is begging me to give in to him. But letting me have this, letting him get what he so clearly wants, means letting go of the past. The heartbreak that has been my motivation since seeing him standing in allegiance with King Outher.

"What are you so afraid of, Sunshine?" His knuckles softly caress my cheek. "Are you scared that you'll like it? Of what he might do if he ever found out? I'm true to my word when I swore to you I'd never let him hurt you again. That I'll rip his heart from his chest if he even dares to threaten you."

"Why?" I'm the one whispering now.

Arthur's hands find their way to my hips, he lifts me with ease, positioning me over him. My hands are on his shoulders, our chests lined up as he looks me in the eye and says with more truth than I could describe. "Because you're the light that's pulling me out of the shadows. The lifeline keeps me from becoming like him–my father. I'm not a good person, Gwenyfer. There are things that I've done and continue to do that would turn the way you look at me into the way you look at my brother. He's the better man. Always has been."

"I don't believe that."

He smiles. "The thing is, whether you believe it or not, it's true. Alex is respecting your wishes. Biding his time, hoping you come back to him. But me," He pauses and stands. I hold on to him tighter, wrapping my legs around his waist until my back is pressed against the wall. "I take what I want. If you were mine, then you'd never cry another tear unless it's from the joy I bring you." He rips my shirt down the middle. "Never feel pain unless it's from too many hours in my bed." His mouth lands on my neck, I moan as he presses his erection into me. "You wouldn't ever have to be afraid, unless it was from the fear of falling in love, again."

I remove his shirt from him, my hands moving to grip his

silky hair.

He stops. Placing his hands on the wall either side of my head. I move to kiss him but he resists. "And because you're not mine, I have to stop."

My eyes widen as my chest tightens, and suddenly, I feel small. "What?"

"If I take you to my bed, you'll never shine the same way you do now. And I can't be responsible for destroying the one chance we have at defeating my father." He places a gentle kiss on my forehead before guiding my feet to the floor, stepping away from me, and heading to his room without another word spoken between us.

Back in my room, after a shower and change of clothes, I sit on the edge of my bed trying to wrap my head around the mysterious figure that is Arthur Penndragon. He's sarcastic, egotistical, rude, and yet, he has a sense of honor. Loyalty and charm that I've never encountered before. I can feel the walls he puts up around himself because they match the same that I have.

I look at my fingertips, remembering my brief lessons with him on that rooftop. His discarded shirt is sitting next to me. I'm not sure why I brought it up here with me. I pick it up, inhaling his moonflower and ash scent. Then feel it before seeing it. Small pink sparks dancing along my opened hand.

My power's back.

I look at his shirt, then at my hand. A few more times before finally piecing the puzzle together.

Alexxander

The thing about working with my brother again is that I can never trust him. He's in there with her, while I have to remain out here until she's ready to see me. Every day I want to go to her and prove that I love her. That I never stopped loving her, but something happened to her while she was in that prison. A shift I sensed in her and so did my dragon. The sooner we kill Outher, the better.

"You're late." I say as soon as I smell him.

"Living with a high maintenance princess will do that." Arthur quips.

I ignore his jab at me. "He's waiting for us. You know how impatient he can be."

"I have the scars to prove it." He says and I sigh. He has every reason to hate me because I'm partly at blame for his painful past. "Get on with it. You know I hate having you be my wings."

"We'll get them back. Just keep your end of the deal. And I'll do whatever I can to help you."

"Shut up." He grumbles.

Flying across the forest with my brother awkwardly holding onto me, is not something I ever thought we'd be doing. I always imagined us up here together. Racing each other against the wind but, like our father has always done, he destroys dreams. And right now, we're on our way to destroy the one thing he's been dreaming about for all our lives.

We land right outside the command tent before entering. The others have gathered around the table with the map of Constellina sprawled out before us.

"Now that the last two members of the Alliance have arrived, we can get started." Prince Lance Obiron, of the Scorpion Court starts. Arthur curses under his breath as he takes his seat next to Merlin Castron from the Arian Court. "We know that the Valerian Princess is in Locknite. And

Princess's Diliha and Gwenyfer are in the fae tree town with Prince Mauris. We'll need to secure more troops if we're going to fight the shifter armies."

"I speak for Princess Victoria." General Mark McCaiin starts. "She would give aid to Princess Gwenyfer without question."

"As will Ombre Court." General Carson adds.

"The only court we're not sure of, is Lirian. Does anyone know what the Prince's intentions are?" Lane asks.

They don't know he was behind the assassination attempt. I go to speak up, but Arthur beats me to it. "Doesn't matter. He'll be dead by the end of day tomorrow."

"How? Why?" Lance demands.

"Because the dumbass challenged Princess Gwenyfer to a duel. And if none of you know her as well as we do, then you should know that he won't come out of it alive." He answers.

He's got a point. "If she kills him, then his court will back King Outher. We can't let that happen." General McCaiin demands.

"If we want the fae as allies, we can't." I comment. "It's the deal she struck with their chief. If she completes three trials, then we have them as friends. There wasn't supposed to be a duel, but the cocky bastard seems to think he can do a better job at representing the human race than she can."

"He has a point. I mean she did run off with a shifter." General Carson chimes in.

"She didn't run off with him. He kidnapped her." Arthur protested, gesturing to me.

"I saved her." I argue.

"From who? Her fiancé, who is now the one fighting her tomorrow." Merlin asks. I bite my tongue so hard I taste blood.

"That's beside the point. Someone needs to talk to him. Figure out his motives and hers. Try to have them come to a mutual agreement so neither one has to die. Maybe they just fight until one yields." Lance suggests.

"Which one of you is staying with the princess?"

"I am." Arthur answers.

Lance nods before speaking. "Good. Speak with both of them. We stand a better chance if we have all the court armies in alliance with one another. Especially if King Outher has magic to his advantage."

The meeting went on to discuss strategy and the flight back to the spot just outside the fae town was quiet. Arthur doesn't say goodbye, he never does. But before he disappears for the night, I leave him with one small request.

"Tell her to fight to win. Not to kill. Even if the bastard would kill her. A man with honor will yield."

CHAPTER EIGHT

Gwen

The steam from the shower swirled around me as I stepped up to the mirror.

Something is different about today. There's this overwhelming feeling deep in my gut that I can't describe. I let out a calming breath. When I step into my bedroom, I see something, rather someone, waiting for me.

I pull the towel tighter around myself, "What are you doing here? I need to get dressed."

He walks over to me, slowly, each step purposeful until the tips of his polished boots brush against my toes. With one hand, he reaches out to gently cup my cheek, tilting my head up so I can meet his gaze. His eyes never drift. His hand doesn't explore and the heat coursing through me is not from my shower. My core clenches at the hungry glint in his jade eyes. No spoken words pass between us, but his thumb brushes my bottom lip. I expect him to kiss me, to claim what I'm willing to give.

"You don't yield. No matter what anyone else says, you kill him before he has a chance to strike you. They want to prevent another war between human courts, but I say fuck them, because if the little prince wins, there'll be a war. The world will burn and every last person or thing he cares about will be the first to perish."

"Arthur," he presses his forehead to mine, "kiss me."

He lets out a breath, "You don't know what you're asking for."

"Yes, I do." I respond, bringing one hand to the nape of his neck.

"Remember what I told you, Sunshine." I nod. "Alexxander is the better man."

"I don't care." Before he can reject me again, I rise on the tips of my toes and kiss him.

It was a soft, quick kiss, nothing like when we struck our deal, but the effect was the same. My skin prickles, and my core clenches. I shudder and press his lips firmer to mine, asking for more. My pulse quickens as those few seconds go by, and for a moment, I wonder if he will push me away again. This is it. The last time I try to explore what's clearly happening between us. After this, I can ignore–

I gasp when Arthur pulls me closer and deepens the kiss. His hand moves from my cheek to my hair, while his other hand grips my hip so hard I know there will be bruises, but at that moment, I don't care. My back hits the wall as he devours me.

"Is this what you want?" He growls hungrily. He lifts me

up as I wrap my legs around him, my core perfectly lined up with his thick erection. I grind against it, seeking that sweet friction. "Tell me to stop."

"Not a chance." Nothing can make me stop.

My fingers find the waistband of his pants, loosening them until I push my hand through to feel him. I wrap my fingers around his thick shaft, smiling with satisfaction against his lips as he shudders at my touch. He's ready, I'm ready, we both want this. Why don't we just get it over with?

"Gwenyfer," he hisses. His hands move to the wall behind my head, but I keep a tight grip on his waist.

"Arthur," I smile at the power I hold over him as I move my hand up and down his length at a steady pace.

"If you don't stop–"

"I'm not going to. What are you so afraid of, Arthur? Ruining me?" He doesn't answer, but the desperate look in his eyes tell me everything. "What if that's what I want?" With my free hand, I discard my towel to the floor, exposing myself to him.

He doesn't explore, but he wants to. I can hear his nails digging into the wall with his restraint. I let him go, reaching up and tear his shirt from him while crashing my lips to his. His hands slide to my back, digging into my skin as he moves us to the bed.

I explore every inch of him. Each scar tells a story of his strength, survival, and his past. I want to know him. I want to know every detail of him and memorize it. This is new, dangerous, addictive and I'm not afraid of it. Of him.

Arthur lowers his pants and I line myself up to his tip.

He hesitated for a moment. "I need you to realize what this means. And I know my brother said the same thing but the difference between him and I, is that I mean what I say. Once this pussy is mine, it's mine. If another man, beast, woman, I don't give a fuck who touches you, they die. Tell me you understand, Sunshine."

There's that desperation in his eyes. He needs to know I'm willing to be his. Forever more, regardless if we're mates or not. Arthur Penndragon would be mine and I his. Although Alex and I went through something similar, it didn't feel like this. Being with Arthur feels like I'm coming alive for the first time in my life. It's like I'd been drowning in expectations, and he's the life raft waiting for me at the surface. I understand now what it means to these shifters to bond with another.

Arthur wouldn't abandon me. He would fight everything and everyone to get to me no matter if it meant his death.

And I will do the same for him.

I slowly lower onto him until he's fully inside of me. We both shudder as we take a moment to breathe, to soak in what we just committed ourselves too.

"I understand, Arthur." I press my lips firmly to his before looking into his eyes again. There's something new staring back at me. I'm not sure what it is until I realize it's a reflection of what I'm feeling in this moment.

"If you don't start moving, Sunshine, I might just combust." He groans.

Our lips meet as I move slowly at first to adjust to the thickness of him. I pick up my pace as his lips explore my body, his tongue moving to each nipple until he wraps his mouth around them, causing me to clench and scream out as he marks me. I force him to his back while continuing to pick up pace. He presses his thumb to my clit while the other remains on my breast.

This isn't about pleasure between us. Or a quick fuck.

We're securing a bond we didn't know existed.

I could feel him reaching for me. Moonflower and ash consumes every part of me, and I wonder if he's experiencing the same thing.

"Gwenyfer," He growls before flipping us and taking control. He picks up a punishing pace, seeking oblivion for both of us. It won't come until our souls connect. Our eyes lock together, every part of our bodies touch as my vision blurs the second my core clenches around him and we both tumble over the edge together.

I see it.

His dragon staring back at me.

It's beautiful, dark, and those familiar jade eyes found mine. In their reflection, I can see my true self.

"You're my mate, Gwenyfer. And now we're bonded for life." Although his dragon is speaking to me, I can hear Arthur's voice. He reaches for me as I raise my own talons to connect to him. Our fingers lace together as I find ourselves back in our human forms, we were back in our human forms. our wings are the only thing exposed. His a shimmering black and mine a deep violet. On each of our forearms, we bear the mark of our mating bond. Pink and golden lightning swirling together as if they were dancing for all eternity.

"You have wings." I whisper.

"You healed me, Sunshine." He responds by pressing his forehead to mine.

"How? I thought there was no way of restoring your power unless you reconnected with them."

"I guess you're the exception to the rule. Mate magic is the most powerful of all." He smiles.

We stay like that for another hour. Connected as we admire our new marks, our new bond. After another shower, we both dress and go for breakfast. But before we step out of the house, I stop us.

"What about this? Shouldn't we hide them until after the war?" I ask, gesturing to the mark.

"Are you more concerned about my brother finding out or the humans?"

"Both. We're already on thin ice with the fae. We need every assurance that nothing is going to stand in the way of us winning this war. We still have to go to Locknite after this."

He nods. "Give me your arms."

I do and he grips each wrist. A spark ignites along my skin causing my hairs to raise as I watch in amazement as my new tattoos vanishes. I look at his arms to see the same happen to his. "Now no one will see them. With the glamor in place, you have nothing to worry about. Well, unless I die."

"Don't joke." I scowl.

"I was only half-joking, Sunshine. The important thing is that we know. And to me, that's enough." He presses a chaste kiss to my lips before opening the door and escorting me to the dining hall.

Arthur

I'm completely fucked.

The crown princess of my sworn enemy is my mate.

I didn't see that one coming. The urge to claim was purely physical and a little cynical at first, just to make Alexxander feel even more pathetic than he already is. But now that her and I are mated, for real, it's different.

All the plans I had at getting vengeance on him and the

humans just washed away the second she became truly mine. I didn't expect to show up in her room as her acquaintance and leave her fated. My intentions were to tell her to kill the bastard prince and deal with the consequences later. But when she walked out in that towel, I couldn't stay away. The thought of her possibly dying did something to me that I couldn't shake. I just knew it infuriated me in an unusual way.

It was her soul calling to mine. She was part shifter, I knew that based on her power but I didn't know she's the rarest of our kind. Violet dragons haven't been seen for thousands of years. which explains why she's experiencing some of the mating powers with Alexxander.

I rub a hand down my face, trying to focus on helping her get ready for the duel. She dressed in minimal armor, a breastplate, arm, and shin plates. They were lightweight but could stop a blunt object.

"I'll be okay, Arthur. I know how to fight." She says, cupping my cheek.

"Go for the kill, Sunshine. Because you know that's what he's going to do."

"Don't worry about me. You've seen me fight. I'm stronger and faster than him. Mauris was probably trained just like the rest of the royal guards in Constellina. I grew up watching them. Sneaking my own training sessions whenever I could. The difference is that I have awakened a power I never knew I had. He won't stand a chance."

Her confidence is reassuring but something still bugs me about this. "You can't reveal your magic to them. Only use it as a last resort."

She nods.

"Princess Gwenyfer, are you ready?" Emanuel asks,

stepping into our little tent.

"I am." I watch her walk away, but quickly grab her arm, spin her around to face me to claim her lips once more. Not a goodbye, but a way of showing what I feel for her. A reminder of who she is fighting for. Of what she is living for.

"Remember what I said, Sunshine. If you die, this entire world burns."

"I know."

Gwen

The fog clears from Arthur's passionate kiss as I step into the middle of a small arena. It's more like a large circle of fae and humans formed to watch our fight.

Mauris wears his court colors and armor, his weapon of choice a spiked mace. This is a fight to the death. Just like in Locknite, there can only be one survivor and it had to be me. Everything is in jeopardy as of right now. To add to the pressure I'm already feeling, I now had Arthur to think about. With the mating bond fresh and new, buzzing through me as I look at my blank arm. Missing the mark.

"This is a fight to the death. No matter how long it takes, only one of you will be named the victor. Any chance at mercy or forfeit, will result in your execution. We fae believe in a fair fight. Do so with honor. You will receive no help from the outside. And upon this agreement, whichever royal wins, the losing court will not go to war with them. If you do, then the fae will intervene." Nefretiri's eyes narrow on each dignitary from the courts. "Begin."

A gong rings as the crowd erupts into taunts and cheers.

Mauris charges at me, swinging his mace directly at my

right side. I spin out of the way, kicking my leg out and connecting with his left side. Quickly turning to face him, I raise my fists.

"If you think I'll show you mercy, you're wrong." Mauris growls.

"At least this time, you're swinging the mace and not hiring someone else to do it." I snap back as his gaze narrows.

That's right you bastard, I know about the price you put on my head.

"What would the other courts think if they knew? What would they do to you?" I bait him and he rushes forward, I duck as his mace misses me by a hair. My withdrawal is swift as each of my blades slice across his face. Not enough to kill him, but strong enough to leave a scar.

We're face to face once more. He touches his cheeks, the evidence of my strike making his face turn red in either embarrassment or anger, or very likely, both. Then he does something entirely unexpected as he throws his weapon aside and gestures for me to do the same.

"You're skilled with those, that I know. But how about hand to hand? Can you kill me without your precious daggers?"

I smirk and toss them aside.

We run towards one another.

He punches out, but I jump, wrap my legs around his neck and flip us. He lands on his back while I front flip to my feet. I move on top of him, pinning his arms down with my knees as my fists begin to fly. I won't stop. I can feel my knuckles splitting with each crack against his face. The sharpened points of his cheek bones impact the smaller bones in my fingers. His blood dribbles out the side of his mouth, yet I still don't stop.

You don't yield.

I wrap both hands around his throat, squeezing and digging my nails in at the same time. His pulse thunders beneath my hand. Mauris tries to buck me off of him, but the way I have his arms pinned, the nerves pinching, causes them to go limp.

"You started all of this"" I yell at him. "When you ordered my assassination. You're the reason this all happened to me! That he took me, broke me, and damn near killed me. I should grant you the death you so rightfully deserve. But I won't." I stand up. He coughs, gasping for air. Walking over to his discarded mace, I lift it and place it next to his head while he is on all fours. His eyes meet mine, his pleas only heard by my ears. The crowd was dead silent as they waited for me to make a choice.

"There is no mercy." Someone shouted.

"Kill him." Another added.

"Do you hear that?" I gesture toward the anxious crowd. "They're calling for your head. And by the laws here, I have to give it to them. But not until you confess what you did. Tell them everything."

He doesn't speak.

I press the spiked ends into the side of his face and he screams out. Tears pour down his face.

"Okay." He croaks out. "I did it."

"Did what?" I snarl.

"I ordered the shifter prince to kill you and I gave the Golden Star to King Outher." He shouts. Not realizing that every ear just heard him confess to treason as not just the court level, but realm level.

"Why?" Diliha asks.

"Because her parents are the reason ours are dead. The sins

of her father should be paid for by his daughter. Especially since he's already dead." He shouts. "You want this whore, this shifter-lover to lead our armies? To become queen? Then you should know exactly who she is and what she's done." Mauris argued to the crowd of dignitaries. "This bitch is a bastard! Her blood is tainted with that of our enemy!"

"What are you talking about?" Another dignitary demands.

"I looked into the family lineage of my soon to be fiancé. Wanting to know who I was marrying and possibly siring children with. Her mother came from Valerian Court. One of their past queens gave birth to a half-human half-shifter child. It was a secret, but I discovered it when I found an old diary of my Father's. He was looking into the legitimacy of their bloodline. I believe that's why he was killed. They were going to persecute your mother and kill you. So your father killed them all. Just to keep your family's secret. Should've known that asking a shifter to kill another wasn't going to work. Clearly, the apple doesn't fall far from the tree."

"Your insults mean nothing to me." I answer in a calm voice. "If you think I'm ashamed of my family's heritage or what I've done, then you're wrong."

"Whore. Shifter loving slu–" He didn't say another word as his head was removed from his body. Not by my hand but by another.

"Arthur? What have you done?"

CHAPTER NINE

Gwen

A pool of crimson gathers at my feet as Mauris's severed head rolls across the floor. Arthur's black talons drip red as his eyes reflect the flames of his anger.

"What have you done?" Emanuel breathes. "He's broken the sacred rules of the duel. Seize him!"

I jump over the body and land in front of Arthur, wielding the mace to anyone who threatens to come near him. He spins around to face the other side. With us back-to-back, we have each other surrounded.

"That was a stupid move, Arthur." I chastise him.

"If you think I was going to let him insult my mate, you've got the wrong impression of me, Sunshine."

They have us surrounded on all sides, the rest of the crowd forcefully pushed back to their homes and guest quarters. I scan their faces, hoping to meet the eyes of the Chief., but she's nowhere to be seen.

"Put down your weapons and allow us to take you without any more bloodshed." Emanuel demands. Arthur won't surrender unless I ask him to.

I square my shoulders, "Only if your Chief promises to let me speak to her without any harm coming to Arthur."

"The Chief will not negotiate with someone who has no honor." He snarls.

"Then there is only one thing left to do." I reply.

A few heartbeats, no one moves. A few breaths inhaled, no one flinches. Someone will make the first strike.

"Ten against two, seems like the odds are in our favor, Sunshine." Arthur whispers.

"If you think we'll make it out alive, you're wrong." I snap.

"Don't be afraid to use your magic. Remember what I told you?" I look at him over my shoulder, his words playing on repeat since he spoke them. My grip tightens on the hilt of the mace as power dances along my fingers.

"If you fight, you will die and all of Constellina will be enslaved to King Outher. Is that what you want? Is that what he is worth to you?" Emanuel asks.

A clap of thunder and strike of lightning tears through the atmosphere as dark clouds loom over us while rain falls. My hair sticks to the side of my face, but I keep my eyes on the fae.

"If you want a fight to the death, I'll give you one. But this is your last chance to walk away." I yell.

"Long live the queen." Emanuel shouts before he attacks.

Without a word passed between us, I stand my ground,

knowing that he has my back as the first fae soldier swings his sword at my neck. I block it with the mace, bringing my foot up to his gut, causing him to double-over, which gives me the perfect angle to impale the spikes in his side. He falls to the ground bleeding. The next one screams a battle cry, throwing a spear at me which I dodge by rolling over and picking up the downed fae's sword. With both weapons in hand, I block the double-swords from another attack coming from my right. Two fae have me pinned, but I hold my position, blocking each of their strikes while trying to find an opening.

My knees buckle, one hitting the ground while the other starts to follow. They're strong, but I'm stronger. I look between the two of them, sword against mace, and sword against spear. Scanning them for any sign of weakness. I notice the one to my left has a scar on his right knee from a recent injury. Using that to my advantage, I kick out while falling onto my back. One fae stumbles backwards, causing the other to lose his footing. I pierce the blade through his gut, the head of his spear coming dangerously close to my cheek.

I push him to the ground, leaving the blade lodged in his abdomen while running at the other. He drops his swords, calling on his fae power. Water swirls around his body like a whip. He sends wave after wave barreling into me. I fall to my knees, trying to hold onto the little breath I have left. Soon, the water surrounds me as I try to swim to the surface, but he keeps adding more. I find Arthur trapped in his own water bubble, fighting against the fae magic like me.

My lungs burn for air. My throat feels like he has a vice grip on it. If I don't get air soon, I'll die.

"I told you, Princess. You would die if you chose to fight. And now, there will be no treaty. No one to save your

C.M. HANO

precious human realm. There is only one person to blame for the upcoming rule of Outher Penddragon, and that is you." I can hear Emanuel's taunts but the only thing I can think about is getting to Arthur, saving him because he can save Tori. I know he'll get her and Diliha to a safe haven away from his father. Away from war.

Arthur. I try to reach him down our bond like I did with Alexxander all those months ago. *Arthur!*

I'm here, Sunshine. We lock eyes through the pool. Our bodies so close, but just out of reach while our souls remain connected.

I don't have a lot of time, but I need you to promise me something.

You're not dying today, Sunshine.

Shut up and listen for once! He doesn't interrupt and before I can lose my nerve, I continue. *When you have the opening, take it. Get out of here, find Diliha, your brother, and go save Tori. Get them away from this war. Promise me you won't let your father turn them into slaves. You have to free them. I don't care where. Just save them for me.*

I can't do that, Sunshine. I can't let you die. That's not how this mate thing works.

I'm the exception to the rule, remember? You told me that. My vision begins to fade, and I know I can't hold on much longer. *Promise me. Now!*

No! Gwenyfer, you don't give up on me. Not now, not after I finally found you.

Goodbye Arthur, tell them I'm sorry.

"Gwenyfer!" Arthur's roar comes with a ring of fire. Knocking all the fae to the ground and breaking us free of our prisons. There is no time for recovery, although I begin

85

to cough up water, gasping to try to replace it with air. "Look at me." His hands are on my face, those dark locks of his sticking to his forehead. Beautiful jade eyes searching for life inside of me.

"Move." He doesn't have enough time to move but I do. Jumping in front of him, I take the arrow straight through my shoulder. I roll a few feet, still trying to catch my breath but then I hear them before I smell it. Snapping my head in the direction of my mate, the fae has him pinned down with iron and a shifter blade to his throat. Emanuel walks between us as I slowly get to my feet.

"You've lost, Princess. Surrender now and I promise he will receive a fair trial. And for the lives of my brothers lost, your punishment will be...merciful." He smirks as if he's won. But what he doesn't know is that my power is surging through me. Prickling along my fingers, waiting for the command it so desperately wants to be given.

"Let him go. Last warning." I demand, in a tone as calm as the eye of this storm. It's only then I realize the rain has stopped.

"If you take one step, you'll force my hand." Emanuel says.

I smirk this time. "Finally answer?"

"Kill hi–" He doesn't get to finish the order as lightning shoots from my hands, hitting Emanuel and the one holding the dagger in their chest. Their eyes widened as they drift to the fist-sized hole I've just left them with. Their bodies fall to the forest floor, dead. The other two shifters back away slowly, their hands raised as I walk towards Arthur, my pink power swirling around me.

When I reach out to him, his fire comes to life and connects with mine.

"A shifter and a human girl that possess the rarest form of shifter magic." I turn around at the sound of Nefretiri's words. "Are you a violet dragon? How can that be?"

I position myself in front of Arthur. "Let him go or every fae that lays a hand on him will meet the same fate as the dead at your feet."

Her eyes dance between us, assessing. Then she cocks her head to the side before smirking, "And he's your mate." She laughs. "Come with me, there is something I need to show you both."

We hesitate for a moment, she sighs. "You're both pardoned. Now let's get a move on. If we're going to save your friends from Locknite and raise an army, we need to move now."

"What do you mean? What about the trials?" I ask.

She pinches the bridge of her nose, as if we're the ones causing problems. "If you are who I think you are, there will be no need for trials. Come with me, please." Arthur interlocks his fingers with mine while staying behind me. "If I get on my hands and knees and pledge my undying loyalty to you both, will that help?"

"No. But I think you know what will happen if you step out of line." Arthur says as I silently agree.

The Chief leads us to her house, through the living room, to a secret door hidden within the wall. We walk down a stone, spiraling staircase for a few flights until reaching another short tunnel that leads to a room full of hanging stone portraits, each one written in the language of the fae.

"What is this place?" I ask.

"The Hall of Prophecy." She answers.

"It's real?" Arthur whispers. Both of us look around the room, each wall lined with prophecies from floor to ceiling.

"Yes, shifter prince. It's very real and so is she." We look in her direction to find her pointing at a stone piece. We move closer and an involuntary gasp escapes me.

"That's...that's me." I say, unsure if I'm dreaming or not. Etched into a prophecy is a picture of me with shifter wings and a crown atop my head.

"What does it say?" Arthur asks.

"When the peace has lasted twenty years, the heir will come. When the realm is soaked in blood and tears, the heir will rise. Find the wings as black as night, fate will come to you. Bear the marks of the father, eyes of green and soul of shadow. For when the heir and nightwing meet, forever will the realm be free. Violet is the rarest form, tempted by the golden one, the heir of now will never be born."

"What does that mean? The heir of now will never be born?" I ask her.

"I don't know the will of the gods, I'm the keeper of prophecies not the interpreter." She answers.

"You're useless." Arthur retorts.

"And you're a dimwitted shifter who almost got the one person in this entire world who can put this right, killed. All because you couldn't stand another man talking shit." She scolds him "Listen, if you're the violet dragon, then that means that he must be the nightwing. If his dragon form is as dark as night, then this prophecy is coming true. Do not let yourself be tempted by the golden one."

"Golden one? There is only one shifter I've ever seen with golden wings." I start to piece everything together, but Arthur says it before I can.

88

"Alexxander, but he isn't the only one." I look at him as he continues. "My father has them too."

"So it could mean either one of them. But, tempt me how?" I ask. "Alexxander's on our side and although he's still delusion about being mates, I don't think he would betray us. What would your father try to tempt me with other than his surrender?"

Arthur scratches his head before speaking. "The relics. We don't know how powerful they all are. Especially if he combines their magic. He could use them as a way of getting you to surrender."

"Then we really need to speak with the gods. Where is the closest temple?" I ask Nefretiri.

"Between here and Locknite. I'll show you on the map, but we still need to discuss our treaty." She reminds me.

"I didn't think we would because of the trials."

"Like I already said, there is no need for them. Prophecy trumps trials. I will grant you my armies whenever you call for me. But remember at the end of this war, who helped you and who didn't. I don't give my secrets away for just anyone." She holds out a hand for me to take, which I do. "It's my honor to meet the now and forever queen."

Back in our room for the night, I've got a bandage wrapped around my shoulder where the arrow pierced through and through. Showered and bellies full of food, I'm ready for a good night's rest.

Arthur went to prepare supplies for starting our journey tomorrow and that left me alone to think about what happened. About the girl carved into stone with wings.

Can I summon them? I think about them, trying to envision them but nothing happens. *Damn.*

I sigh and lay down, pulling the covers up to my neck while letting my eyes close slowly.

Tonight I'll dream of flying. Of winning the war and ensuring the freedom of this realm.

Alexxander

I'm a nervous wreck waiting on Arthur's latest report, wondering if she won her duel, or if she's alive. "Fuck!" I hate being left out of her life. I rip the bark from one tree to the next, letting all my anger and regret pour into them. "Why won't she just let me back in!"

"What did the trees do this time?" Arthur's snide remark has me whirling on him.

"Tell me what happened."

"She won. And we also have the fae Chief's alliance." He answers with a shrug, but something tells me that there is a lot more to his short answer. "You knew she would win, just as I did."

The way he's talking about Gwen is different. A new look in his eyes that's full of admiration instead of toleration. He smells different, his eyes are fuller, skin shiny, and when I realize why, I lose control again. My talons snap out, the tips digging into his throat as I pin him to the trunk of a large oak tree. "You fucked her, didn't you?"

"Seriously? Have you not heard a word she has said to you since she left you standing on the mountains in Locknite?" He demands. Why isn't he fighting me off?

"Answer the fucking question, Arthur. Did you fuck my princess?" I growl.

He smirks. The normal, conniving, uncaring brother of mine. "No, you hopeless bitch. I struck a deal with her, and you know how those go." He kissed her. I'm surprised by the instant relief that gives me. "Then she slapped me because she's very dead set on never falling into bed with another shifter. Dude, you ruined her."

I step away from him, swiping a hand down my face before apologizing. "She drives me crazy. All of this does. I hate not being in there with her, protecting her and trying to rebuild what we lost. I love her, Arthur. More than I've loved anything or anyone in my entire life."

"Even though she isn't your fated?" He asks.

"Fuck fate. Gwenyfer is mine. She's the only one I think about when I wake in the morning, and go to sleep at night. I see her in my dreams but she's fading. Her scent, the memory of her touch. Every day that passes, I feel her slipping from me."

"And why are you telling me?" I shake my head in disappointment. "Oh, because this is the part where I'm supposed to be the good big brother and care about your feelings." He sighs. "After everything that happened to me because of you, you should know protecting her has been the easiest thing I've ever done."

"I know and I'll be forever grateful to you for it." I mutter.

"Are we done talking about your feelings?" He drawls.

I roll my shoulders. "Yes. What does the Chief have planned for her tomorrow?"

"Nothing. We're leaving, heading for the temple of gods then to Locknite to free the Valerian Princess." He states.

"Just like that?" I ask. He nods. "Okay. I'll be waiting for you."

"Gwen wanted me to give you this." He pulls out a folded piece of paper. "And yes, I did read it if you're wondering. Goodnight, baby brother. Happy reading."

My hand tremors slightly as I unfold the parchment. I read it from beginning to end, three times just to be sure I understood what she was asking me to do.

"Alexxander,

Don't be there when I leave this place. Fly ahead and scout for us. I don't want any more surprise attacks if you know what I mean. Leave a bread crumb trail and we'll follow. I've attached the location of the temple. That's where we'll meet you. Thank you for staying loyal to me and to this cause. When we free Tori and defeat King Outher, we'll discuss the status of our relationship further.

Thanks,
Gwenyfer.

CHAPTER TEN

Gwen

The morning we left was eventful to say the least. Arthur woke me in the best way possible.

"Good morning, Sunshine." He whispers before continuing to devour my pussy. His grip is hard on my hips as I squirm against him. Every lick and nip at me brings me closer and closer to the edge. I dig my nails into the sheets, trying to contain my scream as his sharpened teeth nibble my clit before he plunges two fingers deep inside of me.

"Arthur," I moan as he picks up his pace.

"Not until I say so." He growls, continuing to bite and lick, pushing me until my vision begins to blur. "Now!"

Waves of pleasure pulse through me as I scream his name. His lips find mine a second later, claiming me, making me taste myself on his tongue. I wrap my legs down his waist, smiling at the feel of him hard against me. He lines his tip to my entrance and plunges inside of me while I grip his hair hard, pulling his head back until I can sink my teeth into his neck.

He has a bruising grip on my hips while keeping a steady pace, bringing us closer to oblivion together. I pull back to look into his eyes, our pace suddenly slowing as he gently lays me down. Our heated tryst turning into passion. My feelings for him, reflecting back at me in his eyes.

"My mate." He whispers.

"My mate." I kiss him deeply and we shudder, bringing us to bliss. We lay in each other's arms, my head on his chest as I listen to the steady beat of his heart while his fingers trail my arm up and down. I try to find a way to talk about this. About us and what all of this means.

"You're thinking out loud, Sunshine." He murmurs.

"Am I thinking out loud? Or are you looking inside of my head?"

He feigns a scoff. "It pains me to know that you think I would invade your privacy."

"Oh really?" I look up to meet his gaze. "I don't believe you."

He smirks at me, in that smug way of his. I don't say anything as I admire his features. Everything about him is different from the first time I laid eyes on him. From the sharp line of his jaw, to the tip of his nose. Would our kids have his eyes? That causes my smile to fall.

"What just happened?" He asks.

"What do you mean?"

"Something crossed your mind and unsettled you. What was it?"

94

I swallow my fear, knowing I can tell him, and everything will be fine because he's my mate. "What's going to happen when we leave our little bubble?" He sighs, placing his free hand behind his head. "I mean when we leave today. Head back out into the real world where we have to focus on the war and breaking into a prison. Will this go back to the way it was before?"

"You mean, you pretending to not be a love-struck princess and me not caring about you?" He smirks, his tone coated in sarcasm. "If you want to walk out of this room, wearing our mate symbol with pride, I'll do it. But if you wish to keep us in our little bubble, then so be it. You take the lead outside of this room as long as you understand that when the door locks, the roles reverse."

"I think the safest choice is to hide our mate bond until after the war. Especially if we want to keep Alexxander on our side. Some of the royals need to believe that I'm still one of them. A normal red-blooded royal."

He leans over me, kissing my nose before cupping my cheek, "You're anything but normal, Gwenyfer."

"Oh yeah?" I give him a chaste kiss.

"The exception to the rule, the beauty that gave life to the beast, and my mate. Everything about you is extraordinary and I don't know why the gods blessed me with making you mine." Tears swell in my eyes and I don't stop the few that flow as I pull him in for another kiss.

We stay in our room for another hour, committing each other's bodies to memory before getting cleaned and dressed for the long day ahead. Flying isn't an option if we are going to keep our new status a secret. If anyone found out that Arthur had his powers back, there would be a major investigation and it could lead to more trouble than we need right now.

The packs Nefretiri provided us with, carried a few changes of clothes, food, healing herbs, and water skins, as well as a map and bedroll for each of us. The path she drew out for us was heavily used, which she explained would be the case because many fae travel to the temple for worship. But my favorite thing she gave me, is currently strapped to each of my thighs.

"You're giving me these?" I asked as she handed me the two daggers I chose for the duel with Mauris.

"You have a great destiny. And since you intend to keep your power secret until the end, you need weapons you can rely on. Ones you can trust." She explained, while I strapped them.

"Thank you, Nefretiri"" I pulled her into a hug, which surprised her for a moment until she returned the embrace.

She smiles. "Hurry up. The gods don't wait for anyone. Even the violet dragon."

"As much as I love your smile, I hope it's because you're thinking about what I did to you this morning. Twice." He says, bringing me back to the present. The foliage crunching beneath our boots with each step forward.

"And make your head bigger than it already is? No chance." My hand caresses the hilt of each blade. "I was just thinking about my new toys." I unsheathe one, flip it once until the hilt is back in the palm of my hand again and I secure it once more. We continue in silence for a little while, but I figure we have all this time to get to know each other.

"Go ahead and ask, Sunshine." I look at him. "The steam is blowing out your ears with whatever endless amounts of questions you have circulating in that pretty little head of yours."

"Can you tell me more about your family? What happened? Morgan seems to have chosen between the twins at first until I accidentally killed her lover. Alexxander and you have your own issues that we have talked about but didn't give me much to go on. And he told me what happened to your mother. But no one told me why your dad is such an asshole and that seemed to have rubbed off on you."

He doesn't answer right away. "Morgan didn't really play favorites. She wasn't given a choice after what happened." He pauses. "After our mom was killed flying with Alexxander, Outher went on a complete rampage. He almost killed Alex, and I couldn't let that happen. Even after all the shit I've been through, I still wouldn't let my father be the one to end him. He's my brother. Anyway, when I heard what Outher was planning to do to him, I tried to persuade him to stop. To reason with him but he wouldn't listen. The night before his birthday, I snuck out of my room to go to his and get him to run with me.

"We would grab Morgan and just take to the skies. Well, somehow I wasn't as stealthy as I thought I was and got caught right before I pulled the handle. He took my wings, cut them from my body and that's when my dragon went silent, cutting me off from most of my magic. And because I was young and naïve, I believed Outher when he told me that Alexxander betrayed me. Told him that I was plotting against him. For my treason, I was tortured and sent into exile. That is until he needed me to get to Alex.

"After he found out that my baby brother ran off with the human princess instead of killing her, he sent his men out to find me, granted me a pardon if I pledged my allegiance to him again."

"You went back? Why?" I asked, pushing some low-hanging branches out of the way.

"Because of Alexxander." He shrugs.

I stop in my tracks, "Why would you let Alex believe you're evil? That you don't care about him or anyone else?"

"It's safer for him to hate me. If Outher were to ever believe that we reconciled after reconnecting, he'd have a tool to use against us."

"And Morgan? Is she another one?" I inquire.

"I don't know. She's my sister so I should want to protect her, but now that you're my mate and I know she is set on killing you, my loyalty remains with you." He presses his forehead to mine, inhaling my scent and I his.

"He's taken so much from so many people. I promise you that I will do whatever it takes to make this right. Even after they know about us. If the Alex I know is true, then he will accept us. It will take time, but I know he will and as for Morgan, she's grieving. I'd do the same to anyone who killed you. Fuck, I did already."

"I know, Sunshine." He whispers.

"We need to keep going. At least make it to our first camping site before the sun goes down."

"Like I said, Sunshine. Out here, you're the leader and I follow you anywhere."

Arthur

As we make our way to the first site, we continue talking about small things. Stuff I would've never appreciated knowing about someone until meeting her. For instance, she wears glasses but lost them and hasn't needed them since her power awakened. Her favorite sweet to eat is strawberries and cream. And just like I call her, she loves to watch the sunrise.

I watch the warm glow of the fire illuminate her skin. The tent I packed is big enough for us to fit comfortably inside, but my feet will still stick out. Our bedrolls are laid out, while I heat up the stew the fae Chief gave us. She hasn't said much as she organizes our supply packs inside.

I make two bowls and turn around to walk them over to her. Peeping through the slit in the tent, I see her dressed in a silver silk night slip. My throat dries but my mouth waters for something other than the rabbit and carrots steaming in front of me.

"Is dinner ready?" she asks, looking over her shoulder.

"Yes." I go into the tent, and she faces me. I hand over the bowl of stew to her which she greedily eats. "I guess you're really hungry."

"Yeah and you're not?" She asks, giving me a side eye.

"For you." I whisper but not low enough that she doesn't catch it.

"If you think I'm not getting a full night of rest tonight, you're mistaken." She tells me. I put my empty bowl down to remove my shirt. I crawl over her, making her back arch and her nipples brush against my chest.

"What did I tell you about behind closed doors, Sunshine?"

"Does this look like a bedroom to you?" She smiles.

I lean forward, run my tongue down the valley of her breasts, causing her to gasp. "There's a bedroll, a way to secure that entrance, so I'd say yes. Which means I'm in charge."

She hums as I continue to pepper her soft skin with feather light kisses. Teasing and nipping at her until I can smell her growing arousal. I clamp my mouth around her nipple, soaking her nightgown and causing her to scratch her nails down my back. Then I do the same thing to the other. "Does that feel good, Sunshine?"

"Yes." She breathes.

"Do you want me to stop?" I move my right hand to her thigh until I can run my fingers through her soaking folds. Before I can plunge my fingers into her, my head jerks back. A growl rumbling deep in her chest as violet comes to life in her eyes. "Sunshine?"

She pulls harder, then pushes me onto my back with incredible strength. Her fingertips turn into talons as she grips my chin, forcing my head back. "Mate."

The way she is acting reminds me of a part of the mating ritual I heard about but never believed. This is the part where we decide who the alpha is. My dragon rears its head up, calling to hers. "You want to be the alpha, Sunshine? You'll have to earn it."

I flip us, overpowering her for a moment until we continue to roll. Both of us trying to pin one another, nipping and biting, scratching just barely enough to leave small marks that'll heal in the morning. I tear the gown from her body, and she does the same to my pants. My grip on her hair tightens as I have her pinned to her belly, exposing her perfect ass to me. I line my tip up to her entrance and plunge deep inside of her, causing us both to growl.

"I'm the alpha, Sunshine." I snarl, then smack her cheek so hard it leaves my handprint and has her moaning. "Say it. Who's the alpha?"

"You are." She moans as I continue to wreck her pussy. This was going to be quick. The claiming of the alpha isn't meant to be about passion. It's about dominance. My grip on her is hard as I dig my dull fingertips into her skin, adding another mark. We both moan out our release, collapsing on our shattered clothes and rolls.

She flips over, and I wrap an arm around her waist, pulling her back against me. No words pass between us as I listen to her soft breathing until she falls asleep. I pull the covers over her before pulling some boxers on to douse the fire with dirt. Scanning the area with my dragon eyes, I make sure there are no other wandering people near us before locking up the tent and setting up a protection ring around us. A magical alarm system.

Looking back at my mate, I smile before taking my place back beside her. Words I've never spoken come to the surface and I whisper them into the night air. "I love you, Gwenyfer. When this is all over, you'll be my wife. Not just my mate. If you'll have me."

Alexxander

The temple of the gods is extraordinary.

Twelve massive, round columns connect at the top of a long platform of stairs. Each connected by high, firm walls made of gray stone. I land at the top of the steps, right in front of a huge door with statues on either side. None of them I recognize but know in my gut that they're representatives of the gods and goddesses. I raise my hand to grip one of the large golden knockers, but the door opens before I get the chance to.

I take that as my permission to come inside. On the other side, there is nothing except lit torches on each side wall and a single throne at the far end. "Hello?"

My voice echoes as I make my way down the center of the room.

"We know who you are Alexxander Penndragon. Prince of the Dracane Kingdom." Multiple voices ring around the area, but no one is present. "You can't see us. We will not grant you the privilege. For you are a man with golden wings. One of the two that will tempt the fated one."

"What are you talking about? Who? I'm here to–"

"We know why you're here and will not discuss such matters with you."

"Rude." I mutter.

"You must leave Constellina. Go to the lands beyond the seas. Never return." They say.

"If you think you can scare me away from my home, you're wrong." I wait for their response, but it doesn't come. A light beam shines down from the ceiling, and when it clears, the image of a woman adorned in white and gold sits upon the throne. "Goddess, I presume?"

"You presume correctly." She gestures for me to come forward. Not that I have much choice knowing she could overpower me. "You must leave this realm."

"Why?"

"There is a prophecy about you and the fated one." She states.

"What prophecy? Who is the fated one?"

"Too many questions and not enough answers. You have golden wings, do you not?" I nod, confused as to why that matters. "And you wish for your father to fail in his conquest?" I nod again. "Then listen to us as we tell you to leave. Otherwise he will win."

"That doesn't make any sense."

102

"You've always doubted us. And because we've granted you free will, we can't stop you from staying. When you see the imprint of dancing lightning, you'll believe us." She says, then stands to close the distance between us. "You have darkness inside of your heart, Alexxander. Whatever you decide, will turn it to the light or completely to the shadows. Don't be a fool."

Her image fades, leaving me confused at what she could've been talking about. *Father has golden wings. They could be talking about him. Either way, I can't leave her again. My fight is here and now. Gods be damned.*

CHAPTER ELEVEN

Gwen

I was floating on the clouds.

This new mate bond has awakened a fierce desire for Arthur that I can't seem to control. I should be focusing on the mission. On saving my friends from Locknite but my mind is clouded with him.

All these new changes have kept a fresh smile on my face. I know what the next couple of days will bring. And when we meet back up with Alexxander, the little bubble we've put ourselves in will be popped. I awoke to another session of Arthur making my pussy his morning meal. Not that I was complaining. It seemed as though ever since we mated, all I wanted was to feel him inside of me.

Thinking about it now has me clenching. I look around and notice Arthur is a few steps ahead of me. My mouth waters at the thought of tasting him. There's a large tree with foliage nearby, the perfect spot for what I want to do.

"Arthur," I shout.

"Yeah?" He doesn't stop walking. Instead of calling out to him again, I dart to the spot and wait for him to realize I'm no longer behind him. "What is it, Sunshine?" He stops then, glancing over his shoulder. "Gwenyfer? Where'd you run off to?"

He cocks a brow looking for me, then smirks. I squeal with excitement at the thought of him playing my game.

Come and find me. I whisper down the bond.

Playing a little game of hide and scream? He asks, scanning the forest floor for my footprints.

I don't know what the scream part of the game means, but by the smirk on his face and hunger in his eyes, I can figure it out. Only he'll be the one screaming my name.

If you find me, before I get to you, then maybe we'll play your game.

Here's the thing, Sunshine. I always win.

He ventures towards me.

My heart thunders in anticipation. I lick my lips as I watch him move closer. He drops his sack to the ground and leaps over the foliage in front of me. I'm ready, pinning him against the tree, I crush my lips to his while pulling his pants and boxers down. I don't give him a chance to say anything as I drop to my knees and take his cock to the back of my throat.

"Fuck, Sunshine. You could've just asked." He groans and I swirl my tongue around him, pulling him almost all the way out and then taking him back in. I reach up with both hands, one caressing his balls, the other pumping him into my mouth. I pick up the pace, sucking and swallowing until my eyes begin to water. His hands find their way into my hair, gripping it hard at the roots as I move faster. One of my fingers moved to his pert ass, circling the hole. "What are you doing to me?"

It didn't come out as if he were afraid. There was more cursing and groaning as his hips began to move while I let him take control. I breathe through my nose, my eyes meeting his as we connect again. "You don't know how many times I've wanted to stick my cock down your pretty little throat. This is better than any fantasy."

I moan around him then plunge my circling finger inside his ass, moving it in and out at a steady pace until matching his. He speeds up and I can feel how close he is. His cock grows harder, the vein growing thicker until he stops at the back of my throat. I swallow every last drop. When he pulls out of me, I stand, licking my lips before meeting him in a slow passionate kiss. Our tongues mingle as it starts to heat up.

"You want me to fuck you against this tree, Sunshine?" I don't answer him with words as I pull my pants down and spin around so my back is to him. He doesn't hesitate to give me what I want. Gripping my hips and taking complete control while working me into my first orgasm.

"Arthur," I moan as I think about what he said to me last night when he thought I was sleeping. "Arthur, I–"

"Brother?" He pauses as panic seizes me at the sound of Alexxander's voice echoing nearby.

I move to stand then Arthur pins me against the tree, staying inside of me while continuing a slow rhythm. I feel him nip my ear before he whispers, "If you think for one second I'm not going to please my mate, you're wrong. You will come twice before he ever catches us."

Our lips meet while his hands move around my body, one on my clit while the other moves to my ass. Something wet drips against my untouched spot and I feel the tip of his finger begin messaging me. "Arthur, I've never–"

"Let me make it feel good for you, Sunshine." He whispers against my lips, then pushes in slightly while his other hand keeps a punishing pace on my clit. His cock keeps a steady rhythm with the new sensation, I clench down hard while claiming his lips to muffle my scream. He doesn't give me a chance to recover as he adds a second finger and picks up the pace. "One more finger, one more orgasm and then you'll be ready to take me."

I moan, my new talons pierced the bark of the tree as they elongated.

"Arthur? Gwen, where are they? They should've been here by now." Alexxander's closeness has me feeling excited but scared at the idea of getting caught. But all my attention is back to Arthur as he adds the third finger and fucks me into another climax that I have to bite my sleeve to hide. He pulls out of my pussy and ass, but then I feel the tip of him again.

"It will burn at first, but I promise to make it good for you. Perfect in every way. Are you ready?" I nod. Unable to voice anything as I anxiously waited for him. "Play with that perfect little pussy and it will help."

I listened to him and pulled my right hand from the trunk of the tree, moving it to my soaking sex. He pushes in slowly at first and it burns just as he said. I pinch my clit at the same time while fingering myself. Arthur goes a little further rubbing comforting circles on my lower back. *Arthur, if you don't just fuck me, I may die.*

I don't want to hurt you.

I growl in response and he doesn't question me twice as both his hands grip my hips and he plunges deep inside of me in one move. A silent scream escapes me as I look to the sky. The thickness of him stretching me. Uncontrolled tears leaked from me, but I picked up the pace on my pussy while pushing back against him, encouraging him to move.

Arthur understands and picks up the pace. It's all too much. His mouth on my neck, teeth grazing while his hands drift under my shirt to pinch each nipple.

Kiss me, Arthur. Now!

His lips crash against mine in a heated kiss and I feel him explode inside of me while another orgasm tears through me. We slowly disconnect, catching our breath before Arthur grabs a cloth from my bag and cleans me with it before himself. Unfortunately, our moment couldn't last longer as Alexxander is just beyond the trees helping to keep us hidden. Once we're put back together, I look at my mate in his eyes and sigh. I pull him to me for one long kiss, not knowing when I'll get the chance to feel them again.

He presses his forehead to mine and I don't wait any longer to speak the four words that've been circling in my head since this morning.

"I love you, too."

"You were supposed to be sleeping." He smiles and I return it. "We should go."

"Yeah." One more chaste kiss and I pick up my bag before making my way to the path.

Alexxander's back is to me, but I purposely step on a nearby branch to alert him.

He spins around to face me, those blue eyes soaking me

like it's the first time he's ever seen me. I watch his gaze move past me and then his brows narrow. "Where is Arthur?" He sniffs the air then gives me a questioning look before shaking his thoughts away.

Could he smell him? Probably, but why didn't he say anything?

"Taking a piss somewhere. I don't know." I shrug, biting my cheek to stop the smile from forming on my face at the thought of what we just did. I can still feel him inside of me, all around me. Not just in my body, but my soul.

"I hope he hasn't been too dreadful." Alex comments.

"Well, you know Arthur. He does what he wants when he wants."

"You talking shit about me, Sunshine?" Arthur appears a second later and I fight the urge to look at him.

"Always." I respond and then Alex's eyes narrow for a moment. I try to think if I said or did something to give us away but he seems to move on from the topic to inform us of his brief meeting in the temple.

"They said something about me bringing the destruction of Constellina just because I was born with the wings of my father." He runs a hand through his golden locks, clearly stressed. I eye him curiously, noticing how different he is from his brother. There are dark circles around his eyes, and he appears thinner than the last time I saw him.

"When was the last time you slept? Ate a full meal?" I ask.

He shrugs, "Doesn't matter. There is a war coming. Besides, I can sleep when I'm dead."

"Hate to break up our little reunion, but shouldn't we be getting her to the temple so she can have her own conversation with the imperial bastards?"

"Arthur's right. How much further?"

Alexxander points over his shoulder before answering, "Just a half-mile that way. You go on ahead, princess. I need to speak with Arthur."

That doesn't sound good.

"Go on, Sunshine. I'm sure it's nothing more than him pining over you."

"Dick." Alex growls.

"Pussy." Arthur retorts.

"Just don't kill each other. I need you. Both of you." I look between them before taking my leave. Walking from one dragon's den to another.

Squabbling twins I can handle, conniving gods and goddesses, that might be beyond me. The atmosphere on the other side of the large double doors was eerie. I can't see through the dark but remember that I have shifter powers and I know they can. I close my eyes, and attempt to call upon my dragon. "Hello, dragon, if you're listening, I could really use your eyesight right about now."

No response and nothing when I open my eyes again.

"Princess Gwenyfer,"

"The fateful one."

"The violet dragon."

"You've come to the temple seeking answers we will not give. The prophecy is set in stone and what will be, will come to pass."

"If the golden one wins, now and forever will never be."

Alexxander was right about them all speaking one right after the next. "Um, okay. So you won't tell me how to use the magic relics and what their powers are?"

"No."

"The golden one knows."

"Don't let him tempt your hand. If you fail, the realm will fall. And the now and forever will be lost to darkness."

"Stay with the nightwing. Never leave his side, for he is the key to your past, present, and future."

"Leave now, Gwenyfer, the violet one. And never return."

Not wanting to anger the most powerful beings to ever exist, I take my leave, blinking at the bright sunlight. At the bottom of the steps both shifters wait in deep conversation. So focused on one another, that they don't see me approaching them.

"And that's why she will be safer with both of us." I came in at the end of Alexxander clearly arguing to stick by my side.

"Why don't we let her decide what's best for her?" Arthur retorts, pointing to me without meeting my eye. Of course he knew I was there. Our mate bond ignites and grows the closer we get to one another.

"I think our best chance at getting back into Locknite is with Alexxander. He knows it better than you, right?" I ask my mate.

He nods, not meeting my eye.

"Then it's settled. What did they tell you?" Alex asks and I break my stare from Arthur, moving it to Alex.

"Nothing. Basically the same thing they told you." I shrug, not caring if he believed me or not. "But they didn't tell me anything about the relics. Refused, so they were no help, and this trip was pointless. We wasted another week, and I don't know if my best friend is alive."

I push past both of them, pulling out the map to find our location and follow the path to Locknite.

I'm sorry, Sunshine. Arthur speaks to me, but I don't respond. *We'll set her free, I promise. And at least Diliha is safe with the fae.*

I continue to ignore him, not sure what to say to him.

We walk all day and half-way through the evening until finding a spot to settle for the night. I spend my time alone in the tent while the other two tend to the fire and food. Looking up at the sky, I think about what it will be like going back to that place. Is Rosaria still alive? Did she find out who Tori was and if so, did she help her?

The tent flap opens, I know it's Alexxander without even looking. I sit up and silently take the bowl of food from him.

"Can I join you?" He asks, I nod.

We eat in silence, I know he is dying to talk about us, but he won't break the ice unless I do.

"We're friends Alex, nothing more."

"Friends?" He whispers.

I sigh, "We're not mates and what we had was fun but not what being in love was supposed to feel like."

"And how would you know that? You were a virgin before I fucked your tight little cunt." He snarls, anger flashing in his eyes.

"Let's not fight. And besides, that's none of your fucking business. If you wish to stay by my side, you'll watch your tongue and start treating me with more respect. I'm not your mate. I'm the future queen of my court and a heartbroken shifter boy has no right to tell me what I know. If you're going to insult me, then just leave." I snap.

"I'm sorry." He blows out a breath, placing his bowl down. "I've been going crazy trying to wrap my head around how everything changed between us over night. You've had time and space, damn near three months and I have no clue how your feelings could go from love to hate in that time. Now you're saying we can be friends and that at least gives me the hope that you've forgiven me for whatever pain I caused you. Just be honest with me about one thing."

I swallow my next bite, already knowing what he is going to ask and that I'll have to lie to him, again. "Arthur has nothing to do with the way I feel about you or us. You can be my friend, nothing more."

"So, you're telling me that nothing has happened between the two of you? No kissing, touching, or fucking?" I look him right in the face and I see a flicker. He knows something happened and I try to remember every kiss and touch, and fuck. "Arthur told me about the deal you struck with him. I hate that he lied to you about how we make deals. You didn't have to kiss him."

"Right. It's whatever. I'm getting what I want and that's all that matters."

"Gwen," I look up from my bowl. "At the end of this war, once my father is eradicated from this earth, I'd like to start a genuine courtship with you. Since you'll be the queen, I'll assume my father's crown. We could untie the realm under one banner. An unbreakable vow of peace that will last for generations. Don't say no, just think about it."

He takes my empty bowl and leaves me with a pang of guilt from keeping my mateship a secret.

Arthur. I call out to him and in a second, he appears. Securing the tent flap and taking my hands in his.

"He's busy cleaning." I kiss him deeply before creating space between us. "Goodnight to you too, Sunshine. But if you want to sneak off for another tree fuck, just let me know."

"Alex just proposed." I blurt out.

The smile quickly falters. "What did you say?"

"He didn't give me a chance. But I think that when he finds out about us, it's going to be bad. He's still so in love with me, he can't seem to understand that I just want to be friends."

"My baby brother is stubborn, but I promise you he won't hurt anyone you love when we tell him. And when that day comes, I'll gladly shout it from the tops of the mountains." He pulls me into his lap so that I straddle him. His hands squeeze my butt while I begin to shamelessly grind against his growing erection. "You keep doing that and he'll know before you want him to."

"I need you. Inside of me. Now." I demand and thank the gods I had changed into my night slip and robe. Because once he's free of his pants, I sink down on him and fuck him until we're both coming. "Stay with me tonight."

"You don't know how badly I want to but only if we tell him."

I sigh as I reluctantly get off him.

We stare at each other, and I can't tame the lust swirling inside of me. He must sense it because his eyes drift to my parted legs, dripping with his seed. I rub my fingers against my pussy and bring them to my lips, sucking them until I hear his growl.

"Gwen, is Arthur in there with you?" I snarl in anger. Not wanting to give up the chance to have him inside of me again.

Arthur continues his forward progress, plunging two fingers inside my pussy before whispering, "You better answer him, Sunshine."

"No." It comes out surprisingly steady.

"Right. Well, goodnight."

"Goodnight." Fuck. This feels too good. He lowers his mouth to me, adding his tongue to the motion bringing me to another orgasm which I muffle.

His lips meet me in a hungry kiss as I shred his clothes, along with my nightgown. I wrap my hand around his hard cock and flip over on my belly, begging for him to take my ass again. "I need more, Arthur.."

I'll never be full of you, Arthur. Never stop wanting you.

Fuck, Sunshine. I was just thinking the same thing.

He's going to hear us, and I don't fucking care because I'm your mate and your mine. Our dragons, souls, bodies, we belong to one another. Now and forever.

I lift back, taking him deeper as I turn my head to claim his lips, matching him thrust for thrust.

Harder, Arthur. I'm so close.

Me too.

Bite me. Mark me. Claim me.

His teeth sink into my neck, and I whimper my release into my hand as he draws blood, his seed filling me. We come down from our high, collapsing naked against the blankets, but he doesn't pull out. I don't want him to.

We're in our little bubble again. I let out a sigh. "Arthur, I want to see it. I know it's there, I can feel it, but I need to see it."

He knows exactly what I mean and the second the glamor disappears, a deep growl resounds in the tent. But it doesn't belong to me or my mate.

Alexxander

When she answered me, it didn't sound right. I slowly

unzipped the flap and what I saw happening on the inside paralyzed me at first.

They were together. Naked and he was alpha mating with her. I knew they were lying to me. I'm not a fool. How could someone resist her? But seeing his cock plunging in and out of her has me wanting to rip his throat out.

I watch until they climax, ready to interrupt their little facade. As soon as I step through the flap, I see their arms light up like the evening stars. A mating imprint on their forearms, matching the exact symbol the gods told me about.

My heart shatters at the betrayal.

A predatory growl escapes through my gritted teeth, capturing both of their attention.

"Alex, we can explain." Gwen says as she begins to pull her night slip back on.

"She's my mate. My true fate." Arthur says and as soon as I lock eyes on him, then look at their imprint once more. My dragon comes to life.

The sound of bones crunching and clothes tearing resounds in my head. My human form disappears into the beast I was born to be. A burst of flames releases from me, burning the tent to the ground. Another dragon's roar booms, it's one I recognize but haven't heard in nearly twenty years. I spin on my hind-quarters to face him.

His piercing jade eyes are the only thing I see when his midnight scales blend with the night sky.

"You're not the only one with power now, baby brother." He snarls.

"Good. This would be no fun if you were still a weak shifter."

CHAPTER TWELVE:

Gwen

Fuck.

Claws and teeth.

Flames of red and green dance across the sky, leaving streams of smoke across the stars. I can barely see Arthur, but Alexxander's golden scales shine as bright as the constellations above. A part of me feels as though this is all might be my fault; but the other knows that who I decide to welcome in my bed is not up to Alexxander.

Their roars thunder across the land. Anyone for miles could see or hear the two dragons locked in a deadly waltz of wings and flames. Anyone who knew them would recognize the princes.. And that's what we don't need.

"Stop fighting!" I shout to the skies, but it's pointless. They wouldn't be able to hear me over their own insistent shit talking. I look around for anything I could potentially use to get their attention, but all I have are the sticks from the campfire, our sacks, and my night slip. A sigh escapes as I close my eyes, concentrating on my dragon.

Please work this time. I claim you, rare violet one. Make us one, allow me to shift. Nothing happens. I think about the first time I saw her. It was the moment I connected with Arthur on an intimate level. When our mate bond sparked, and we accepted one another. Our dragons, powers, imprints, everything that made two people fated, came to be. I focus on what I was feeling in those moments.

Vulnerable and secure.

Ecstasy and passion.

And mostly, alive.

My eyes snap open, my vision sharper than ever before. I feel my nails transforming into talons as I fall to my knees. The pain from my bones crushing and reforming coaxes a scream from my throat, but the human voice is replaced with a beastly roar. The ground quakes beneath my claws, the wind breaks against my wings as I stretch them wide, getting used to the new sensation.

New scents surround me. Everything is brighter, louder, the bees buzzing five miles from here seem ten feet away. I can see the small stream cutting through the brush fifty feet from us. And the sound of claws and teeth, scent of blood, have me taking flight. I'm clumsy at first, but my instinct kick in and soon I'm darting between them. Knocking Alex's clamped jaws from around Arthur's neck. He rolls a few feet back until he rights himself.

I remain between them, narrowing my eyes at the golden beast while keeping my mate behind me.

"No more." I snarl.

Alexxander moves a little closer, his dragon eyes assessing me. "You're the violet one?"

I look down at my new limbs to see the beautiful dark purple of my scales glinting in the moonlight. "Stop this and we can talk."

"You have lied to me about so many things, Gwen." Even in the deep tone of his beast, I can hear Alex's sorrow. "You should've told me."

"I know, but I'm not going to apologize for finding my true mate."

His eyes snap behind me, connecting with Arthur's, but I move into his line of sight. "If you want to be pissed at someone, it should be me. I told him not to tell you. Besides, Alex, I've been telling you for months that we would never be together again. If you want to fight, to release all that built up anger and pathetic jealousy, then it will be with me. I've beaten you once and I can do it again."

He growls and Arthur growls back in my defense.

"You're wrong about one thing, Gwen." I prepare myself for his attack. "You may have beaten me in my human form, but you've shifted for the first time. I'm stronger, older, and faster. Move out of my way so I can finish this, once and for all."

"Not a chance." I snarl, the need to protect my mate surfacing. "Get on with it. Attack me, prove the gods correct and tempt me with a fight to the death. I'm sure they told you that if I fail, Outher will enslave the realm. Is that what you want? King Outher of Constellina?"

I watch as he thinks for a moment, steam rolling out of his nostrils. Slowly, he descends. I follow, keeping Arthur at my back as I tell him without words to let me handle this. Once we land, the shift back to my normal human body is just as painful. Arthur quickly throws my robe over my naked body, hiding me from view as Alex glares at the two of us.

Alexxander stands at a distance, his clothes perfectly intact, something I guess I need to learn at a later time. He rubs his chin as I slowly approach him. The ground is cold beneath my bare feet, but I keep going until there's only three feet parting us. I wait, giving him the opportunity to speak first.

"What do you want me to say, princess?"

"That you understand. If anyone would know what finding your fated mate feels like, it would be a dragon shifter."

His fists clench at his side, "That's the thing, though, I thought I found her. I never thought…" he pauses, shaking his head before finally meeting my eye. "You looked me right in my face and told me nothing was going on between the two of you!" Alex's eyes flash with fire as he continues to yell. "You could've told me! Instead, you decided to rip my heart out by fucking him in the next tent over from mine! You were supposed to be mine!" Tears well in my eyes over his pain. "You don't get to do that. I don't want your pitiful tears, Gwenyfer. After everything we went through, I gave up my family, my position and power, for you!" He shakes his head. "No, not for you. For an ungrateful human whore that spread her legs for my brother. You fucked him before he was your mate, I know you did because you did the same with me!"

Arthur appears at my side in a flash, ready to kill his brother for insulting me but I stop him. "We hurt you and I'm sorry for that, but I'm not apologizing for falling in love with the one I was meant to be with. We never were, Alex. That's what I've been trying to tell you since Locknite." He laughs a little then turns on me, but Arthur catches him by the wrists, their dragons coming to life. "Enough. I won't let you kill each other over me. We have more important things to worry about."

"She's right, brother. Swallow your pride, go find something to sink your cock into, and then remember whose side you're on." Arthur warns.

Alex's eyes shift between us before he jerks his hands free and takes a defeated step back. His wings burst from his back before he snarls, "I hate you. I'll never forgive either of you for doing this to me."

Then he's gone.

My knees give out beneath me.

The weight of the incident crashes through me as tears fall.

Arthur wraps me in his arms, calming me as I let all the guilt in.

"Don't cry over him, Sunshine. He isn't worth your tears."

I look at my mate, unsure why he doesn't realize the gravity of Alex's loss. "He was our way in. He was the way to rescue Tori from Locknite. Now he could go to your father and tell him everything. All our plans, the prophecy, and the fae." I wipe my face, stand, and go to the tent, though Arthur isn't far behind me. I numbly dress before packing. "If we leave now, we might be able to get to Locknite before he betrays us. Now that we can both fly and there's really no one to keep from knowing our status as mates, we should get there in two hours."

Arthur doesn't say anything but wraps his arms around me, preventing me from moving. "Stop stressing. My brother just needs to blow off steam. He's in love with you, Sunshine." He spins me around to face him, gripping my chin to meet his eyes. "If you ever left me for another and I saw his cock claiming what's rightfully mine, I'd want to kill the fucker too, but I wouldn't betray you to my father."

"What if he does?"

"You just let me worry about my baby brother, Sunshine."

We slept for a few hours until the sun began to rise. We cleaned and packed after eating a quick breakfast. Arthur's wings stretched wide from his back. Those dark scales glistened in the rays of light peeking through. It almost gave it a purple tone. "Are you sure about flying?"

I let my violet wings stretch behind me. It took a few tries, but I was able to just call upon them like I do my talons. The tearing of clothes comes with learning the magic of the shifter. That's what Arthur explained to me last night as we were falling asleep.

"Let's save a princess."

The journey to Locknite didn't take as long as I thought it would, despite going slow so I could adjust to my new wings.

Last night, fully shifting, was different because I reacted out of emotion and the need to protect Arthur. Now that our emotions aren't running high, we can relax. Or at least that's what Arthur is trying to get me to do. But something is off. Alex left when he was pissed off and heartbroken. He could be telling our enemies everything and when we walk into Locknite, it will be a trap.

"Stop thinking out loud, Sunshine. My brother isn't that foolish."

"I can't help but worry about him. I've never seen him that angry before." I kick a stone from my path. We landed about a mile from the bottom of the mountains, deciding it would be safer to finish the rest of the journey on foot to not alert the guards at Locknite of our presence. They'll have increased security since then if they're smart. "Tori isn't just my best friend, she's my family. A sister I never got the chance to have growing up and if anything else happens to her because of me…I couldn't live with myself."

"We're going to get her out, I promise."

"You can't make false promises, Arthur!" I snap because ever since we mated, he's been more on the optimistic side of things, and I really miss the other side of him. "What has happened to you?"

He cocks a dark brow.

"Don't look at me like that. You used to be more fun." I continue my forward progression, not wanting to give him time to come up with something more positive to say that would just annoy me. He remains quiet, keeping his distance a few feet away from me. I stop and so does he. "I'm sorry. I feel like the weight of the world is crashing into me and you're just trying to make me feel better."

"I call you Sunshine for a reason, Gwenyfer." He closes the gap between us, interlocking his fingers with mine. "I was dark and twisted on the inside before I met you. You broke the ice that was covering my heart. And when we mated, I finally saw the light again. After years of bitterness and revenge, you gave me a new purpose." I look down at my feet, but he lifts my chin. "I'm here to follow your lead. Now and forever."

"Even on days when I attack you for no reason?" I whisper-ask.

"Even on days when you stick those little daggers up against my throat and fuck me until the Sun circles the earth, Sunshine." I smile and push up on my tiptoes to kiss him. "Now, let's go save your friend and kill a king."

Alexxander

I was on a warpath.

My blood boiled through me as the hurt of her betrayal and the image of my brother's cock deep inside of her, had me wanting to kill something.

I don't know where my blind-flight took me, but I ended up in a small village tavern near Locknite. The place was nearly vacant except for a few patrons and the bartender. She shot me a smile while pouring a draft for another customer. When she walked over to me, I couldn't help my eyes from going to the sway of her hips. My cock jumped at attention. I haven't been buried in pussy since the last time I fucked—

"You look like you could use a drink." She said.

"I could use more than that." I responded with a smile.

She looked down at her watch, then back at me, checking me out from head to toe. When I flashed her a smile, she winked at me, walked over to the top-shelf liquor, and poured us both a double-shot. It went down smooth, and I gestured for another.

Five shots in, I made my way to the bathroom. While washing my hands, the door opened, and I didn't notice who it was until I heard the lock slide into place.

"You shouldn't be in here." I said as I looked at the bar

tender.

"If you're going to try to convince me that you weren't giving me fuck me eyes, then I need to take another shot." She pulls her white shirt off, exposing her breasts wrapped in lace. "What'll it be? You want to drown your sorrows in more tequila?" She shoves her skirt off, showing me she is completely bare underneath. "Or me?"

I watch as she hops up on the counter next to me, opens her legs, and begins rubbing her pussy. I jump at the opportunity because I need it. But I don't want to look at her. Taking control, I grip her hips and force her to her knees, shoving my dick right to the back of her throat. I'm not gentle. She's choking by the time I pick up speed.

Her nails dig into my ass, and I can hear her begging to breathe.

"Take my cock, like the whore I know you are." I growl. Her teeth clamp down and I rip her to her feet. Spin her around, slap her ass and then shove my dick into her pussy just enough to wet before claiming her ass. It's not tight and from the moans, I know she's been fucked plenty of times back here. I close my eyes, imagining that it's Gwen instead of this cunt. My dragon mating with hers. Claiming her once more. "You were mine. Fuck!"

I grunt as I pull out and paint the bartenders back with my seed.

Then I'm gone before she can realize what just happened.

On the balcony of my sister's apartment, I look inside to see her fast asleep on the couch. I wrap my knuckles gently on the glass and she awakens. Her eyes meet mine as she approaches the door.

"What are you doing here?"

I swallow hard. "We need to talk."

CHAPTER THIRTEEN
Gwen

"I don't remember it being this far up." I pant, nearly out of breath.

"We could always fly." Arthur suggests from ahead of me.

"And alert the guards that we're here? Not a chance." I shout back. My legs burn, I clearly need to work on my endurance and stamina. Regardless of having these new powers, I'm still half human, and that part of me doesn't like climbing up a steep rocky side.

We make it to a stopping point to rehydrate and I swear somehow, a rock got in my boot. Sitting on a boulder, I pull both off and shake them out until the damned things are clear. I scan the area, just to see if I can remember the exact spot I landed when Alex flew me out past the prison walls, but nothing is coming back. I push my feet back into my shoes and stand, trying to get an even better view.

"How close are we?" I ask.

"Not sure. Should be coming up soon since this is the same spot where we made our little deal." He smirks.

"Right. Then that means we still have about another half-hour to climb before we make it to the point Alex dropped me off at." I throw my sack back on and with a determined step in my foot, keep moving forward.

"You should relax, Sunshine. By the time we make it inside, you may not have the energy to perform our little break out." Arthur says.

"Yeah, well do you think Tori gets any breaks?" He doesn't answer. "The faster we get there, the sooner we can get back out. There is a war going on and as the leader of the Sagittarian Court, it's my duty to protect those citizens. I don't think Lord Regent Warren is doing that. If it were up to him, he'd probably hand the keys to the Queendom over to your father the second he made a deal. The conniving cowardice fuck."

"Such a foul mouth for such a high lady." Arthur comments with a little humor in his tone. "But then again, I love what your mouth can do."

"Rescue my best friend with me and I'll show you exactly what I–"

"Please don't finish that statement." I stop. My heartbeat growing faster, hands inching to grip my daggers as I blink twice before looking at him. "Did you think I was going to break my promise to you, princess?"

"Alexxander, you're back." I clear my throat but don't move my hands from the hilts of my blades. "And *why* are you back?"

He sighs. "Because I told you, I would do whatever it took to free Princess Victoria and take down my father. This is part of that."

He's showered and changed into more appropriate clothing for a mission of this magnitude. Relax fit pants and a button down with a vest, his golden locks trimmed just a little shorter. "And when did you have time for some rest and relaxation? You were gone for twenty-four hours."

Arthur's question matches my own as he steps up to his brother. Their resemblance is uncanny to a stranger, but after getting to know both of them, aside from their hair and eye color, I would know who is who.

"I gave myself time to think and cool off. I'm here to help you, not to fight." Alex answers. I look deep into his eyes, ones I used to be able to read so well. They seem different. He's off and not his usual self. Could that be because of what we did? Of the prophecy? "I'll swear it with blood."

I look to my mate who doesn't seem to trust his baby brother, that makes me not want to either. "What are you trying to prove, Alex? Even if you make the oath, saying words in whatever exact manner we ask you, how do I know you won't find a loophole? How can I ever trust you, even a little to do this? You're not one to control your temper. Jealousy isn't something you erase from your personality with a shower and clean clothes. You saw me and your brother together. Found out we're true mates and now, you are okay with it? It doesn't make sense."

"I can be the man you think I am." He sighs and moves closer. "We were close once, princess. Give me a chance to prove to you that I'm still on your side. Regardless of the personal situation between you and Arthur."

My gut tells me to stay away. To not trust him because of everything that has happened in the last year. But, we also need him to get us back into Locknite. "Swear you'll get us in and help us find Tori." I state while drawing a dagger, cutting it across my right palm and offering to do the same to him. "Swear your allegiance to me."

He hesitates for a moment, then grabs the blade and copies what I did before handing it back to me. I clean it off on my pants, sheathing it before looking at him and connecting palms. We wait for him to make his oath. In a blink of an eye, he jerks me towards him and leans down, I lean away from him. "There was a time when you wouldn't pull away from me."

"There was a time when I trusted you. You betrayed me once, Alex. Don't think I've forgotten." He smirks at me. "You're not my mate, Alex. I have no desire to kiss you or be in your arms." It didn't come out harshly. But hurt flashes across his face, along with something else. An emotion I can't seem to pinpoint. "If you wish to help us, you have to promise me you'll do what I asked."

"Get you in and save your friend." He repeats it and I nod. "Then I swear that I'll help you get into Locknite and free your friend." A zap of magic buzzes up my arm, sealing his oath with blood.

We break apart, Arthur pushing past Alex to pull me into a deep kiss and give me strength to heal my hand. He tries to make it last longer than it should, but I know that's just to spite Alex. "Stop it. We need him."

"Sorry, Sunshine. Actually, no, I'm not. He needs to know who you belong to." Arthur growls intently, flashing a look to the man in question. "But for your sake and Victoria's, I'll behave."

"The entrance is just below there. We'll need to fly down

in order to make. Climbing would give away our position because the rocks are slippery." I stand next to Alex and look where he's pointing. "We should make it down in about five minutes. Just be ready to fight, there may be guards."

"I didn't think anyone else knew about the wall?" I ask.

"Well, just to be on the safe side." He states.

We make it down in the time he said we would. No guards on lookout which should relieve me but makes me more anxious. Alexxander places his palm against the wall, and it dissipates, just like last time, only there's a prison hall on the other side.

I let out a breath and take the first step inside, Arthur and Alex at either side of me. It's dimly lit and quiet. Not a prisoner or guard in sight. The evidence of what happened here three months ago, is gone. It's as if nothing happened at all. My gut starts to churn and the hairs on the back of my neck raise in alarm. I freeze.

"What's wrong, Sunshine?" Arthur asks.

"Something's wrong." I whisper. We both scan the area as my eyes shift into my dragons. I move slowly, trying to keep my head on a swivel, looking anywhere for any sign of danger. Nothing happens so we keep moving.

We make it around another corner before stopping. "Where's Tori's cell?"

"From the intel I gathered, she'll be in the highest part of the prison." Alex answers.

"Which means?" I inquire.

Arthur answers this time. "She'll be in the dark tower."

"That doesn't sound good."

Alex leads us around some more empty halls until landing on an elevator. "This will lead up to the Warden's level. He's the only one with access to the tower aside from King Outher. We'll need his blood to get int."

"Where are the guards, Alex? The prisoners? What's happened here since we left?" I keep asking and he doesn't answer with words. "If this is a trap–"

"I'll gut you." Arthur finishes.

"I made a vow, princess." He responds, unusually unbothered by Arthur's closeness of me. "You'll see your friend soon.

I pull my blades and Arthur does the same as the elevator brings us closer to the top of Locknite. It dings and there's a brief moment when I think I see something in the haze of my current reality. But then the doors open, and we walk into a large open space with nothing but furniture laid out. I check it out and notice a desk that appears to be for an assistant but it's empty. Then I realize it. *"I'll help you get into Locknite and free your friend."*

I whirl on him in a flash. My daggers forming an 'x' against his throat as my dragon snarls at him. "You set a trap, didn't you?"

"He didn't." I know that voice. "But I did." Morgan snickers as I look over my shoulder to find Arthur pinned to the floor in iron with a shifter blade to his neck. "If you think that he isn't over you, you're wrong, princess."

"You said she wouldn't get hurt." Alex chimes in and I snap my attention back to him. But my position with my blades doesn't falter.

"I should slit your throat for this."

Morgan approaches me with a cat-like smile, "Do it. Those blades will only render him unconscious for a few minutes. You know the only true weapon is what is next to your mate's throat."

I jump off Alex and charge at her, but something blocks me, knocking me off my feet into the wall. I try to move but can't. Lettie, the one who kidnapped Alex and tried to turn him against me. She utters incoherent wards while using her powers to keep me paralyzed. "Get those fae blades away from her." Morgan orders.

My grip is so tight, I can feel the fabric imprinting in my skin. I'm no match for Lettie's magic and I feel my hold on them loosening as her essence grows stronger. They clatter to the floor as I close my eyes, thinking of the last possible thing that could help us.

Shift. Please dragon, our mate needs us.

"She's calling on her beast." Lettie tells Morgan.

"Bind her. And then we will continue this little chat while we wait for the king to arrive." Morgan's words go without any protest and one of the shifters she came with soon has me clasped in iron on the floor across from my mate. We lock eyes as I try to reach him down our bond but it's cold. There's nothing but silence.

"How could you betray us?" I yell at Alex. He looks away as if he's too ashamed to meet my eye. "You're a fucking coward, Alexxander Penndragon!"

Morgan claps her hands and laughs before walking over to where I've been forced to my feet. We meet eye to eye, and she cocks her head to the side before her fist connects with my gut, knocking the breath from my lungs. She takes a handful of my hair and brings her knee straight into my jaw with a crack. I spit my blood to the floor as the involuntary tears fall. "This is the hero of the human race. Pathetic, if you ask me."

"I'm going to kill you for touching her!" Arthur snarls.

"Oh, brother, I forget about you." Morgan smirks as she makes her way to him. I jerk against my chains when I see her take the weapon meant to kill his kind and cuts his shirt open. She presses it into his skin. "Father told me how you got these scars. It's really inspiring. I learned a lot from his recount, and I might practice with you later."

"You're dead. So fucking dead!"

"Oh, stop with the theatrics." She snaps. "You may have gotten away the first time, little princess, but not this time. No, there will be no one to save you. And your friend, Victoria, was it? She's dead."

"No, you're lying!" I shake my head in disbelief. My gaze shifts to every other person in this room until finally landing on him. Alex, the one who told me she was alive, then Arthur, the one who told me when she had been captured.

"I'm not. Look, I recorded the entire thing." Morgan puts her phone up to my face as the video plays. It's of Tori and Rosaria in the arena, being forced to fight. I have to force myself to watch just so I know if she made it out or not. Rosaria easily overpowers her, and my heart shatters. In between my old cell mate's jaws is my best friend's heart. "Told you. Poor thing didn't last a week."

"You've been lying to me this entire time." I look at Alex who still refuses to meet my eye. "Look me in the face, you fucking coward! All because your brother is my one true mate, you decide to throw a temper tantrum and run to tell your little sister everything? Then lie to my face about my best friend still being alive. You've proven to me the kind of man you are, Alexxander Penndragon, and I'm blessed to know that the gods made the right choice in not choosing you."

Alex finally looks at me, "She was alive the last time I saw her. I never lied to you. But you seem to have forgotten a lot of things about me while you've been living in the fantasy world with my brother." He approaches, Arthur's chains rattle as he uselessly tries to get to me. "I never have, nor will I ever lie to you. You betrayed me, Gwenyfer. And I should thank you because you reminded me of who and what I am. The fucking mafia king and prince of the Dracane Kingdom. Now that I'm done with you, there is nothing left for me to lose. To care for. So, I got you in just as I swore I would, and I freed your friend."

"She's dead." I say through clenched teeth.

He shakes his head. "You failed to mention the name of said friend." The doors to the elevator open and my mouth drops open. "I believe you two were old cellmates. Became friends right before you escaped."

"Rosaria?" I cry out.

"Hey, Gwen. Sorry–" Morgan strike's her across the face to silence her.

"She's free just as my brother swore. You wanted to get back here so badly; it was the perfect set up. You chose the wrong brother, my dear. Arthur wouldn't have betrayed you but he wouldn't have helped you either. Alex, on the other hand, knows what it means to be a part of our family." Morgan drives that invisible knife deeper into my chest.

"When I break free of these chains, you'll be the first to die. And then," I turn my head to Alexxander. "You're next. When the war is over and your father has fallen, I'll present him with both of your heads before he joins you in the afterlife." My threat becomes a promise to myself, my mate, my people, and my best friend.

Morgan strikes me across my face, her talons scratching my cheek causing me to bleed and wince. "You won't be getting out, this time. Lettie will see to that. I sure hope you enjoyed your little powers while you could."

"What are you talking about?" Arthur demands.

"Father will explain everything. For now," she feigns a yawn. "I'm bored. Throw them somewhere until the king arrives. Bring in the next two fighters. I'd like it to last until round two this time."

The guards force Arthur and I into separate rooms, chained away from each other while continuing to follow the rest of Morgan's commands. I curl into the corner, bringing my knees to my chest and laying my head on my forearms.

"You okay, Sunshine?" Arthur's voice is soft, and I wish I could curl into his warmth right now.

"No." I whisper.

"They'll die. I will stop at nothing until I have them dead at your feet, Gwenyfer. Do you hear me?"

"I failed, Arthur."

"No, you haven't."

"Don't let the golden one tempt me...yeah, I was tempted and now look at us. Locked in a place where we have no allies. Our powers are useless and..." I sigh. "What's going to happen?"

"I don't know but Outher won't kill you right away. He'll find some way to use you." He answers.

"Right." I let the grief of my loss take over as I sob into my arms. Arthur growls in anger and pain as he's not able to comfort me. "I love you, Arthur Penndragon. No matter what happens. Just know that."

"Don't talk like that. We aren't saying goodbye." He stretches his chains as far as they can go, reaching for me as I do the same. Our fingertips brush and it causes a shiver to move throughout my body. "We'll get through this and then we'll burn them all."

"Tori's death will be avenged." I add.

The door slides open, and we look towards the man entering. "Ah, isn't this a nice little surprise? My traitor son and his little whore. From what I'm told, you two are mates." His eyes shift to our where our imprints mark us. "Well, fuck, this just brings me even more good news."

"Let her go, Outher." Arthur demands.

"Why would I do that? Now you get to see what it's like to have the love of your life ripped from you." Men charge inside, taking me into custody. I fight them the best I can, managing to break their hold until I can run into Arthur's arms, our lips connecting in a deep kiss that doesn't last long enough.

"I'll always love you." Were the last words he said as hands drag me from his arms.

CHAPTER FOURTEEN
Arthur

I fight as they rip her from my arms.

The iron chains creak against the strength of my power.

"There's no use, Arthur. She'll die and you'll be free from the hold she has on you." Outher says while patting my face, adding insult.

He looks directly in my eyes, victory shining brightly, but he doesn't know the bond we share. Even in death, she'll be mine. "You better kill me too."

A moronic laugh escapes him as a devilish smile paints across his face. "Is that so?" I nod. "Here's the thing, Son. You and the little princess have no power. No magic. No ally in these walls. Your brother came to his senses about her, and you will too." Outher grips my wrist, stretching my marked forearms out to examine our bond. "These will begin to fade and everything you feel for her...well it will be as if it never existed."

"You're delusional, Outher." He raises a brow. "No one has magic strong enough to erase a mating bond. It isn't possible. I'll never stop loving her."

Outher lets his grip on me fall as he rolls up his sleeves, showing a faint design of crimson flames dancing with emerald. "She was taken from me too soon and with each year that passes, this goes with it. One day, there will be nothing left, and the memories of your mother will be gone with it."

"You're a liar. That's not possible."

He smirks, sympathy lining his brow. "My son, the one who thinks he knows everything but fails to realize he knows nothing. Shifter magic comes from an ancient source. The same source as the beings we all thought went extinct thousands of years ago. I believe you and Gwenyfer met their current leader while on your little tryst." I try not to react, but he catches it. "Oh yes, Alexxander has told Morgan everything. He just didn't know that I was listening in the other room. Isn't it crazy what heartbreak and alcohol can do to a person?" He sighs, as if he's bored with this conversation. "You'll spend a few days here with nothing but the longing of your mate to keep you company. When I feel you're ready, we'll transfer you to another room. One where your lessons will begin."

I spit in his face, hatred for him growing deeper by the second. "Make me a deal, Outher."

He wipes his face and meets my eye, curiosity blooming to life. "Why would I make a deal with someone who has nothing to offer me? I have your princess, three of four relics, and the fall of Constellina right in my pocket. What could a worthless traitor have that would make me give up his mate?"

Before I lose my nerve, I say the one thing no shifter has ever dared to say. At least to my knowledge. "I'll give you everything. My powers, wings, fuck even the clothes on my body. You just have to promise me that she'll be untouched."

"She truly does have your mind boggled if you're willing to do something as foolish as give up what makes you a shifter. No. I will not have my son become a mortal human over a girl." He snaps.

"Then kill me right now because every person that touches a single hair on her head will die. And when it's your daughter and son laying at your feet, you'll know deep down you had the chance to prevent it. To stop the Barringer of death from getting to them." I snatch him by the throat, digging my dull fingers in as tightly as possible. I feel his heart beating steadily beneath my palm. "I swear this to you Outher Penndragon, your bane is coming. By the claws of the *Nightwing*, you will fall. When this story gets told, the scholars will read about the false shifter king who was foolish enough to go against the strongest dragon to ever exist."

"I'm the strongest dragon, boy." His talons dig into my wrist, drawing blood as he pries my fingers from around his throat. "The *Nightwing* doesn't exist. There is no dragon stronger than the *Goldwing*." He creates distance between us before opening the door, with one last breath of words to leave me with, he says, "The sooner you figure out the winning side of this war, the better it will be for all of us."

The door slams shut as a roar breaks through my throat. "I'm going to kill you Outher Penndragon!"

As the days passed, Outher's promise of loneliness and longing came true. A dull pulsing pain crept up my arms, increasing in intensity every second. Ten seconds passed, then another ten. The pain would soon become unbearable. Surely this pain would stop soon. Surely there's an end to this. I wasn't so sure and ready to give up because of it. I paused for a moment and took a deep breath. Perhaps if I could shift my focus away from the pain, it'd be easier to manage.

I was growing tired. Tired both because of the pain and tired of having to deal with the loss of our connection, but I didn't really have a choice in the matter. I told myself it'd be over soon, whether that was true or not was irrelevant as it gave me the necessary strength to deal with it.

Gwen...I reached for her. Every second of every day, I called her. On the other end of our bond was nothing but a wall of thick ice. Keeping me from her and her from me. My dragon was quiet. Weakened by the iron binding us to this wall. I picked up the loose screw I'd found and drew another line. The only way to tell the time was the rise and fall of the sun's rays from the small windows at the top of the side wall.

Seven days in the dark.

Seven days apart.

Seven days of starvation.

Seven vows of deadly devotion.

A promise of vengeance for not only me, but for her. I sang those verses on repeat because I knew he was watching me. That they were keeping a close eye on their prisoner. They'd be foolish not to.

The lock in the door turns but I don't acknowledge it. Too weak from the lack of food. Morgan and two others walk in, the men hoist me to my feet, but I'm dead weight in their arms. I feel my sister lift my head up to look at me. "You're pathetic, Arthur. If it were up to me, I would let you starve to death, but for some reason father still has a soft spot for you. Bring him to the dining room. It's time for a family dinner."

I'm dragged back to the elevator that brought us up. I can see my reflection staring back at me. My arms are limp, knees bent awkwardly, and eyes half-sunken from lack of sleep. The rise and fall of my chest is spaced out longer than it should be. I know that the end will be near. It won't matter if she isn't alive and unscathed. The bell dings signaling the arrival of whatever floor we land on. I feel the tips of my boots drag across the carpet as I keep my eyes glued to the teal carpet.

The guards force me into a seat, connecting the ends of my chains to bolted claps on the floor. My head hangs low, though the aroma of food makes my stomach growl in pain and hunger. I don't know who is sitting at the table, and frankly, I don't care.

"Arthur, you're not looking too good, son." Outher comments. I don't give him the satisfaction of a reply. "Perhaps this will help. Bring her in."

Her? He couldn't–

"Arthur?" I hear Gwen's voice and look up, wondering if I'm dreaming or if this is some sick hallucination brought on by lack of food. She's beautiful. I want to reach for her but can't seem to move. "May I go to him?"

I look at the man she's seeking permission from, and he nods. Her soft hands cup my cheek, and her eyes meet mine. She smells clean, of soap and perfumes. "Have they hurt you?"

"No, not at all. They've been nothing but kind to me." She says and I'm taken aback at those words. "Arthur, if you listen and do as you're told, he's promised to let us go."

I search her eyes, not wanting to believe the words coming

out of her mouth. I look at her fully, but find she's no longer in her usual attire of pants and a shirt. Instead, she's dressed in a regal gown of cobalt blue with gems sewn into the dropping neckline. My gaze drifts to her arms but they're covered, and I need to see that this is truly her.

"Show me your arms." I speak softly, my voice hoarse thanks to the dryness in my throat. Gwen doesn't move, stunned by my request. "Now, if you want to prove to me that you're really you."

"Do it, Gwenyfer." Outher orders and she doesn't hesitate.

"Look, see? It's me." Her beautiful skin is painted with our mating bond. A choked breath escapes me. "I know. Listen, we need to talk–"

"After dinner." Outher interrupts. "Take your seat, my dear. We shall enjoy this family meal together."

The cover for my plate is removed as my mouth begins to water at the roasted duck breast sitting at the center of potatoes and beans. A cup of water is placed within my reach, and I sip on it slowly. Not wanting to cause any more pain to my insides than I already feel. Father sits at the head of the table with Morgan and Alex on his right, Gwen, and I to his left. Her presence next to me soothes the ache from our bond. I slowly pick up a potato and pop it into my mouth. A groan escapes me at the burst of flavors. Butter, garlic, salt, pepper, and a little earthy flavor from the golden skin.

No words pass between us as we each eat in silence. The clattering of utensils is all that can be heard. When I've finally had enough, I reach under the table to interlace my fingers with Gwen's. She snatches her hand from mine. I give her a confused look, but she doesn't acknowledge me.

I scan the faces of my so-called family for any clue as to

what is really going on. My stomach clenches, I grab the arms of my chair as my insides feel like they're on fire.

"Arthur, are you okay?" Alexxander's false concern would piss me off, but whatever they did to me has me doubling over. My knees impact the hard floor, the crack radiating through my body. "What the fuck? What did you do to him?"

"Lesson number one, Son. Never show sympathy for the enemy." Outher preaches as the pain begins to subside. "Get him back up."

When I'm righted again, I look towards my mate who appears to be completely unaffected by what just happened to me.

This isn't right. Gwen would be launching herself over this table ready to stab them.

"What's wrong, brother? I thought you'd be overjoyed to be reunited with your one true love?" Morgan snickers.

"Where is she? Where's Gwenyfer?" I snarl.

"She's right next to you." Outher answers, cocking his head to the side. My chest feels tight as I claw at it, my eyes burning which causes my vision to blur.

"That's not Gwenyfer, that's not my mate." I protest, standing as I grip the edge of the table just to have something to hold on to as my world spins.

After a few seconds, the image clears and I find myself face to face with Lettie. We're in a dark cell and directly behind her, strapped down bleeding and unconscious is—

"Gwenyfer!" I shout.

"You came out of that one quicker than I anticipated." Lettie comments. My eyes narrow on my mate, every cut and open wound making me fight the restraints keeping me chained to the table.

"Gwenyfer, wake up!" My voice chokes when I can barely see the rise and fall of her chest.

"Arthur?" Her voice is so weak, it pains me to see her like this. To know I failed to protect her. "What are you doing? I thought you loved me." She cries and I realize she's dreaming. Only, if it's anything like what I just experienced, it's a magic infused hallucination.

"What did you do to her?" I snarl at the woman who used to be my mother's best friend.

"She's going through the same training as you. Only, her mind is easier to break than yours now that you are at full power." Lettie responds while walking over to a table lined with different devices. She pulls a golden needle.

"She'll see through your lies. Our bond is stronger than any Fae power you have."

Lettie walks over to Gwen, pushes the needle directly into the crevice of her strapped down body. My mate doesn't flinch or scream. But I do. I know what Fae needles do. They extract power while leaving the soul weakened.

"Outher will be disappointed again. I don't understand. If she's a mate to you then she can't be human. We've seen her magic." Lettie curses to herself and that gives me hope. "Unless," she turns towards me and looks me in the eye before asking, "what is she?"

"Who?" I deadpanned.

"Your mate, asshole. What kind of creature is she? If Fae magic doesn't work on her, then she isn't a shifter."

"I don't know." I answer honestly, trying to hide my own curiosity at this revelation.

"I see." She goes back to Gwen, withdrawing the needle coated in blood and brings it to one of her specimen jars.

Dropping the blood inside before coming to me. "I haven't had the chance to use these on you yet. Per the king's instructions, but maybe he doesn't have to know."

I feel the point pressing into my arm, the pain slowly building deeper until it connects with bone. I scream. Then she enacts the spell, speaking the Fae words to remove my arm essence. "Tell me what she is, and I'll return your power to you."

Lettie tries to shout but I can't hear her over my own roars. "Fuck you!"

"Fine. I have ten more just like this one." She jabs another and another until she only has one left, but before she can speak her next words, a flash of pink lighting bounces off the walls. Lettie doesn't seem to notice as her focus is on pushing the last needle right between my eyes. The spot is known as the access point to a shifters dragon. "Your dragon will speak before letting you both die."

My vision fades in and out but I'm conscious enough to watch what happens next.

"Awaken dragon of Arthur Penn—"

Her words are cut off by the claw sticking out of her mouth, blood dripping on the floor as her throat is clutched in the tight grip of my mate. Gwen's power comes to life as pink consumes Lettie's body, turning flesh to ash.

She looks like a goddess.

"Arthur," her hands hold my head up as she turns it from side to side, assessing my injuries.

"The needles." I whisper. She goes to work freeing me from everything. We fall to the floor in a tangle of limbs, neither of us wearing anything except undergarments. "Is it really you, Sunshine?"

She frantically nods and presses a kiss to my lips, deepening it as I feel her pouring her strength into me. My wounds slowly heal as I kiss her back until we're breathless and letting our bodies do the rest. We lay on the cold floor, facing each other with no words passing between us.

"Seven days, Sunshine. How did you manage that?"

"I thought about you and everything we've been through over the past three months. When they tried to fool me, there were things that helped me realize that it was a fake version of you. Their image of the person they think you are." She whimpers.

"Same, Sunshine. Have we been in this room the entire time?" She nods. "Fuck."

"Lettie used a lot of magic on you to keep you and your dragon subdued. If she didn't, you would've overpowered her. She tried to use you against me, but it didn't work. When I saw her turn those fucking needles on you, my dragon came back to me."

I kiss her with a newfound hunger. She moans as she presses closer. We're weak and covered in blood but we need this. I pull her panties down and find her soaking for me. She grips my cock and pumps me a couple times until pulling my boxers down. I wince in pain as I try to sit up, but she takes control.

She sinks down on me, kissing me while she moves slowly. My hands go to her hair to anchor her and slowly, with her help, I sit up. She removes her bra, giving me access to her plump breast. I clamp my mouth around one, marking it. Her pace quickens slightly, and I move a hand between us to find her clit, pressing my thumb to her as our mouths connect.

When we're close to the edge of release, my dragon

connects with hers. Just like when we accepted each other as mates.

"Arthur." One word spoken, a million more behind it.

"I know, Sunshine. Me too."

CHAPTER FIFTEEN
Gwen

Day One:

The cell I was placed in was just like the ones back at the palace.

The only difference was it was a cage, with bars on all four sides built in the center of a room. Across from my temporary living quarters was a metal table that looked like it was used for torture. A shudder ran down my spine, causing gooseflesh to pimple my skin.

Arthur was my main concern at this point. They already took Tori and Rosario from me which meant I needed a new purpose. A way to keep me sane for however long I was going to be stuck in here because this time Alexxander was on their side. I knew no one else would come for us. The other courts were busy with the war and Nefretiri, so I had no way of contacting her.

I pace around the room, thinking of all the possible

scenarios that could happen now. Would he torture Arthur in front of me as a way of getting me to give him what he wants? Or is he going to strap me down and try to get Arthur to betray me? No, that would be too obvious and neither of us would do that knowing we would have more to lose giving him what he wanted. Arthur may not have other people he cares about outside Locknite, but I do.

I sigh, slinking down to the cold stone floor as put my head in my lap.

I'm sorry, Tori. I should've been here sooner.

A tear escapes me, but I wipe it away because crying won't bring her back. This is going to kill Diliha. I hear the main door open and jump to my feet. Walking in with a smug smirk on his face is Outher Penndragon with his little posse strutting behind him. Morgan finds a chair to sit in and Lettie begins unrolling items across a flat countertop mounted perpendicular to the strap-down table. The shifter king approaches me, his eyes assessing from head to foot before he laughs.

"I mean, when I came face to face with you again, I thought you'd be a worthy opponent." He sighs and shrugs. "Ah well, beggars can't be choosers, can they, princess?"

"Where is Arthur?" I bite back.

"He'll be here soon. For now, I'd like to ask you some questions." He replies.

"If you think I know something that you don't, then you're mistaken."

He snaps his fingers, and a guard brings him a chair to sit in. I watch as he makes himself comfortable, folding his hands in his lap and then begins with his interrogation. "Where is the last relic? And once I have all four, how do I use them?"

I can't answer that. Mainly because I simply don't know.

But even if I did, I wouldn't tell him. "I know that you went to speak with the gods, Gwenyfer. Alexxander also spoke with them. He said you told them about the prophecy, but he seems to think there is more to your conversation with them then you led on. Why don't we make this easy on everyone and you tell me everything I want to know?" He attempts to add a charming smile. In a way, I can see a resemblance of his younger son, but not Arthur.

"If I knew anything more, which I don't, then why would I give you that power? Go to the temple and ask them if you want to know so badly." My tone is calm. There is no use in wasting anger and rage on him when I can't reach him beyond these bars. "Did you stop and think for one second that your precious baby boy might be leading you astray?" Outher narrows his eyes, "Think about it. He has every reason to double cross you. You're the reason his brother hates him. The one who had people do unspeakable things to him when he turned eighteen. Blames him for his mother's death and, there was one more thing...made him lose the woman he loved."

"She does have a point, my king." Lettie added.

"Give her food. We'll continue this tomorrow." They all make haste to leave except for the one person who slides a tray made of food underneath the bottom bar.

The plate has something that looks like creamed potatoes and meat that is burnt. I lift the food up to sniff it, then grimace. It could be laced with poison and that's not something I'm willing to risk. My stomach is in knots from everything that happened today. I have no desire to eat.

I find a spot on the floor, lean against the corner, and rest my head on the cool metal. Looking at my forearms, I run my fingers across the imprint as a heavy sob builds in my chest at the loss I feel for him. I know he isn't dead, but I can't feel him. Every time I reach down our bond, I get blocked by a wall of frost. My dragon hasn't made an appearance since they clamped iron around my wrists.

We'll get out of this.

Day Two:

Morning came with a splash of ice water against my face.

I cough and clear my eyes while standing. "You people really love doing that."

"Good morning to you too, princess. I see you didn't eat last night, a mistake you won't make again. I assure you." Outher states while Morgan unlocks the cell door and two of their men come inside to retrieve me. "Don't fight them, you have no power here."

The shifters stare me down, but I don't falter. Raising my chained fists, I give them everything I have, punching and kicking until they have my arm locked behind my back. If I move any more my shoulder will pop out of place. I'll be rendered helpless. My breathing is heavy, and my head is dizzy, but I won't stop. *You don't yield.* Arthur's words have stuck with me since he spoke them.

"I'll never stop trying to fight you." I snap.

"We'll see." He sneers.

They bring me towards the table. But at the last second, push me down into a chair. My chains rattling as I jerk my arms free of their hold. The door opens and I look over to see two more men dragging in Arthur's unconscious figure. He's only wearing pants and there's blood painted across his body from obvious cuts they made. In less than twenty-four hours, they've managed to add more scars to him. I charge at the closest person, tearing into their neck with my teeth. The metallic taste of his blood coats my tongue as he screams and we fall to the floor. Someone pulls me off of him, but it's too late.

"Restrain her." Morgan commands.

I lock eyes with Outher and spit the victim's blood at his feet. "If you think this will break me, you have no idea who I am."

Morgan brings a shifter blade up to her brother's throat, waiting for her father's orders.

Outher takes a seat next to me, in the same relaxed position he was in yesterday before he eyes me curiously. "You'll let her torture him just to save a few fae? They are not your friends. If they were, then wouldn't they be here right now attempting to rescue you?"

I don't listen to his lies. He has no idea what Nefretiri has planned. We have no contact with one another, and she has no way of knowing we failed. "Arthur wouldn't want me to give up my, only leverage I have against you. And if you're here, trying your best to get me to betray the fae, then that means you're scared of them."

"Scared of who?" He chuckles. "Some tree loving worthless creatures?" He leans forward, gripping my chin before moving it to my hair to grip it hard. "I fear no one. Especially you, little princess. You're forgetting one thing; I know how the bond works. Even if it isn't today or tomorrow, you will break because the one thing fated mates can't stand is seeing their lover bleeding and in pain."

Arthur groans in pain, catching my attention as my heart

sinks the second his eyes meet mine. It's for a brief moment before he fades out again and I bite the inside of my cheek, trying to fight the words Outher so desperately wants to hear.

"Begin." Outher commands as I watch while Lettie slices, pokes, and magically tortures my mate right in front of me. It last hours and I nearly lose my will until finally, Outher gives up for the day. "This is what it will be like for the both of you until you start giving me answers, little princess. Just remember that you have the power to stop this. All of it."

"Fuck you." I snarl.

He smirks, insultingly pats my head, and walks away. I'm thrown back in my cage while they take Arthur back to his and leave me alone with slop for food. I resisted eating for the first three days but at one point, I was too weak to move. My body needs the sustenance to stand let alone fight. It didn't taste bad, but it didn't taste good either. It was something to give me energy, and I needed to have enough for both of us.

Day after day, it was the same routine. Retrieve me, strap Arthur down, torture him, and then leave. I didn't break until we hit day seven. There was something about all of this I didn't understand. What power or tool were they using to keep him subdued? He didn't react to most of the things anyone else would. How were they doing it?

On night six, curled in a ball on the floor, I closed my eyes and let my mind drift to memories of my loved ones.

"Happy birthday Gwen!" Tori squealed as she bounced on the edge of my bed, handing me a brown box with a golden ribbon tied around it.

"Seriously Tor? You didn't need to get me anything." I said, but I knew I might as well open it and give her the satisfaction

of being the first to give me on my sixteenth birthday. On the inside was something I hadn't expected to come from her. Two beautifully crafted daggers with diamond encrusted hilts. The blades were dull and I knew she did this for me so I could wear my favorite weapons for ceremonial reasons. Most of the men at court had a designated sword, women weren't permitted but the rules don't apply to me. "They're beautiful."

"I had our court blacksmith make them for you." She informed me.

"Alright, now how the heck am I going to top those?" Diliha chimed in but handed me an orange box..

"Come on, D, you know I'm going to love it." I smiled and went to open it. Staring back at me was a silver hairpin that doubled as a weapon. It matched the daggers in every single way except the point would cause harm.

"I figured you would still want protection even when you're at those boring ceremonies." Diliha said.

"I love you both, very much. Thank you." I pulled them both in for a hug, overjoyed from the generosity of my best friends. A knock sounded on the door and in came one of the guards.

"Pardon the intrusion, Your Highness, but this was delivered for you." He states. In his hands was a dark blue box wrapped in pink silk. I take it, the weight of it heavier than I expected. After the guard leaves, I walk over to the bed and eye the tag curiously.

"Who's it from?" Tori asked.

"Yeah, I thought we were the only ones who celebrated your birthday." Diliha added.

I don't answer them because my heart is in my stomach and tears swelled in my eyes as I read who it was from. "My parents."

"What?" They both said at the same time.

"Do you two mind if I open this one alone?" I ask, although I know they would give me privacy without protest. Once I was alone, I moved over to my desk and slowly unwrapped the box. The silk ribbon holding a familiar feel to the kind of fabric Mother used to wear. I let out a breath before lifting the lid open and removing the paper on the inside. There was a letter from them.

Dearest Daughter,

It's your sixteenth birthday and if you're reading this, that means we've left you before we wanted to. And trust me, darling, we didn't. You're going to become of age soon. Ready to take a husband and rule the Queendom just like I did. I know an arranged marriage sounds terrifying, but it worked out for your Father and me. Slowly, I began to fall in love with the man behind the title and what a good man he is. There are important things I wish I could be there to tell you about and someday you'll understand what that means. For now, I want you to do whatever it takes to stay alive. Because this world needs your bright light shining in it. Without it, we would all fall to the darkness threatening it. For your birthday, this very special day, we have given you the gift of power and knowledge. There are four relics, stars if you will, given to certain courts for protection: Golden, Frozen, Autumn, and Crimson. Each one holds a special essence from the gods and goddesses watching over us. My warning is this, if the four be as one, all magic shall be undone. Protect them at all cost, for if they fall into the wrong hands, Constellina

will fall again.
We love you,
Happy Birthday
Mother and Father.

The tears kept falling, and I looked underneath the parchment to find a silver star-shaped locket. Opening it, I gasped at seeing what was inside.

Snapping awake, I touched my neck, remembering the spot where I used to hold the last gift my parents ever gave me. "Mother was right. She did give me the gift of knowledge." I whisper to myself recounting the dream. "He doesn't have the real one."

A victory smile and newly found will washed over me as I let myself fall to my dreams again. Inside my locket was the only secret I would go to my grave keeping. No matter what happens Arthur would want me too.

Day Seven:

"I will tell whatever you wish to know so long as you make me a deal. A blood deal with no loopholes or misconstrued words." Outher was sitting across from me as he did the last week.

"What made you change your mind?" He asked.

I feigned a sigh and played the heartbroken mate, "You were right. I can no longer stand the sight of him in pain. All I want is to heal him and ensure he is safe."

The shifter king's gaze narrows, locking onto me for a few moments, searching for the deceit but nods. "Then so be it. You tell me the terms of your blood deal and I will tell you mine."

"You swear to let Arthur, me, and Rosario walk out of this prison healed, fed, clothed, armed, and most importantly, free. Then you leave us alone. Don't have any of your pets follow or attack us."

"Is that it?" He asked.

"Alexxander," I start, "He stays with you and never leaves your side again."

"It's a trap, my king." Morgan sneers. "Clearly her and him have concocted some kind of plan to keep him close enough to kill you."

"What makes you suspect that?" He turns to ask her.

"Because it's what I would've done." She answers.

He rubs the stubble along his jawline before elongating a talon and slicing his right palm. I reach across and allow him to do the same to me. Our hands join and he speaks the terms of his side, "You have to tell me where the fae are located and the last relic. Where is the Crimson Star?"

"The Crimson Star is exactly where all of us believe it to be." I answered.

"In the heart of the Scorpion Court." Outher whispered and I nodded. "And the fae?"

"Bring me the map and I will draw a circle right where they kept me." His eyes alight with joy and I squeeze his hand. "Do we have a deal?"

"I swear it. Gwenyfer, Arthur Penndragon, and Rosario are to be healed, fed, clothed, and freed from Locknite. None of my soldiers, allies, or guards will follow or attack you." He stops.

"And Alexxander." I growl.

"Alexxander Penndragon will never leave my side again."

With the final word of his oath, magic buzzed between us, causing a burning sensation to trail up my arm.

"Thank you for your cooperation, little princess." He goes to release my hand, but I dig my nails in deep, using whatever strength I had to jerk him toward me to speak words low enough for only him to hear.

"The Barringer of death is closing in on you Outher Penndragon and she's closer than you think."

Arthur

I awoke in a small bed in a room remarkably similar to the tent Gwenyfer and I shared.

"Sunshine?" I shook the daze out of my head and sat up, flashes of what happened at Locknite causing my chest to seize. Looking down, I'm dressed in new clean clothes, all black as I preferred. I unbutton my shirt and notice no new wounds and my head throbs with confusion. Black boots and socks sit at the end of the bed. I put them on and make my way outside.

The sun is bright, and I blink to clear my vision. Headquarters in the Fields of Constellina. It must be early morning because the camp is unusually quiet, and I see no one around aside from the guards posted in the lookout towers around the perimeter. I make my way to the main tent where all our council meetings have been taking place and see it's empty.

"Where is everyone?" I whisper, scanning the area to find one familiar face. I look down at my arms, rolling up the sleeves, relief floods me as I find our imprint is still there, shining bright.

"Sunshine, where are you?" I reach down our bond, expecting to hit that block but then I feel her as she responds.

"Come and find me." She flashes an image of her in a hot spring and I groan at the need to touch her. To be inside of her and consume every part of her.

"Good morning, Arthur, glad to see you finally on your feet again." Prince Lance comes up to me with a biscuit and a cup of coffee in his hands.

"What does that mean?" I ask.

"You've been asleep for two weeks. Princess Gwenyfer never gave up hope that you'd awaken." It seems like my mate has a lot of explaining to do.

"Do you know where the nearest hot spring is?"

He points to the far east side of the camp, "About five miles into the trees."

I don't wait for him to say another word as my wings come to life and I take off. It's unstable at first and I feel like a teenager who just got control of half-shifting again. When I balance out, it doesn't take long to find the heated waterfalls. I look around for her, my arm buzzing with how close she is. Then I see her. Breaching the surface, her tits on full display as she pushes the water from her eyes. My cock springs into action as I shred my clothes.

A territorial growl rumbles in my chest as I make my way to her, my wings still exposed until I have her lips against mine. I hoist her up as she wraps her legs around me, giving me the perfect angle to insert myself inside her. My wings act as a privacy screen as I fuck her. Our tongues dance as she moans and digs into my back. I graze my teeth against the soft skin of her neck, licking until I bite and suck, causing her head to fall back.

"Arthur," she moans.

"So responsive, my mate." I growl against her skin.

I reach between us with one hand, my other holding the weight of her and find her clit. The need to feel her clench around me is unbearable. I move at the pace and rhythm that always sends her over the edge and soon she's screaming my name while milking me as I spill my seed into her.

We hold on to each other, our foreheads pressed as we breathe in each other's scent.

"What happened to us, Sunshine?"

She lets out a heavy breath go as she unwraps herself from me. "We should get dressed. I have a lot to tell you about."

After we're dressed, we find a shady spot underneath a large oak tree and I listen as she recalls the events of Locknite. "And I made a blood deal with him. That was the only way I was going to get us out of there with our powers intact."

"But that's not what I remember. You killed her." She shakes her head. "Was it all an illusion?" She confirms it with a silent nod. "I didn't know Lettie was that powerful."

"Neither did I, but it doesn't matter. This is real. What we just did, coming together again after three weeks, was real." She says as she places a hand on her beating heart. "I'm so sorry for letting it go on for so long. I was going to give up. I was ready to let him take my powers if it meant you were no longer in pain."

"What stopped you?"

"My mother." I cock a brow. "It was a dream or a memory I had on the last night we were there. I remembered the gift she and father gave me on my sixteenth birthday. And Arthur, you're never going to believe what it was."

"The key to my father's destruction?"

"Not exactly, but, and I haven't told anyone else this yet."

"Spit it out, Sunshine."

"I know where the true Golden Star is. Your father has a replica, powerful somehow, but just a fake." She practically squeals out.

"Could that mean the same for the other two?" I ask.

"I don't know. Diliha might know but Tori," she stops, choking on a sob at the name of her late friend. "We'd have to go to their courts to find out. And Lance is still alive, so either Outher hasn't figured out what I meant when I told him the little riddle, or the blood oath is preventing him and his men from coming here."

"Then we know what must be done." I kiss her, unable to resist trying to take all her pain away. "Call the banners. We need to find out what everyone knows about each relic. First, speak with the Scorpion Court Prince. If we can get all the relics, King Outher will not win."

CHAPTER SIXTEEN

Gwen

We take our seats around the table, Arthur to my left and Lance to my right. When we got back to camp, there was no chance to have a moment to speak with him in private about his relic. I will bring the topic up, but I'll be vague about it.

"We finally have the Sagittarian Court Princess in our presence. All courts are represented aside from the Lirian Court. Where is Prince Mauris?" Prince Lance asks.

"He's dead. I killed him." Arthur announced. A chorus of whispers from the others in the room rippled through the room. "Before you royal dickheads get your balls twisted over this, you should know that he brought it upon himself. I have my reasons and owe none of you an explanation. The important thing to know is he was a traitor and an ally to King Outher. Now, we don't need him or his army to win this war. We have something much stronger."

"Ha. What can we do to beat shifters and mutated humans?" The Regent from Valerian scoffs.

"You tell them, Sunshine."

Right. "Well, we all know about the relics given to certain courts to guard for protection." They simultaneously nod. "What if we can get a hold of them and use them against the shifters? It would give humans an advantage because even the great Outher Penndragon can't fight against the power of the gods."

"You're forgetting one thing. He already has three of the four. To include the one from your court." The regent from Diliha's court answers. "And what about yours, Prince Lance?"

We all look at him, and he nods. "It's safeguarded. Outher cannot find it because very few know of its precise location."

"There you have it, princess. We can't use one to fight against three plus shifter magic." Another lord I don't know adds.

"Are you saying all hope is lost?" I ask. They don't answer. I stand, placing my palms on the table, and lean forward, garnering their attention. "King Outher will not win this war. We have all the power and knowledge that he thinks we don't. There is one ally that hasn't arrived yet, but should be here soon. And once she is here, she'll tell you they have the strength and numbers to give us the advantage. Princess Diliha will arrive with her and as for the relics, leave that for Arthur and I to handle. Once the wall of Illusion completely falls, the rest of his armies will march across the fields and meet us sword for sword. Ensure your soldiers are ready at any moment. The fight for Constellina will begin."

The meeting continued as we discussed strategy.

Once everyone left except for me and Lance. I snatch the opportunity to discuss the Crimson Star. He pours a cup of wine for each of us as I sent Arthur away so Lance wouldn't feel so intimidated. They haven't seen our imprints, nor have they asked what our relationship is, and I appreciate it. Now isn't the time to explain to them that I have shifter blood as well as fated to one.

"The silence is awkward, Gwenyfer. I know you wish to ask me about my relic."

"Yes. Is it where I suspect?"

He sips on his wine before answering. "At the heart of my court?" He chuckles. "That would be too simple to solve. No, it's hidden and the only person who knows where it is has long since been dead."

"What? Who? Why didn't they pass the knowledge down to you, the heir?"

"Probably because they didn't have any warning before they were slaughtered." It clicks the second he answers. I see a reflection of my own sorrow in his dark gaze. "If I knew where it was, don't you think I would want us to find it and use it against those shifter bastards?"

"Yeah. Do you have any clues where the last place it could have been seen?" I inquire, not letting this go because knowing that I can have the Golden Star and possibly find the Crimson one we'll have at least two.

Lance thinks about it for a moment before setting his cup down and going over to a desk lined with miscellaneous papers. He reaches into a draw, "This is something my parents left me. Gifted it to me on my sixteenth birthday with an encoded message I could never solve. I was too afraid to ask for help because it was meant for me. But something about what you said has me wanting to see if you're right about clues."

He stands after pulling out a small metal box and approaches me with it.

"Did they give you a letter with it?" I ask.

"Yes. How did you–"

"My parents did the same thing." I murmur.

With shaky hands, he opens it to reveal a ruby encrusted locket in the shape of a star. "I haven't been able to open the actual locket. There's a key or spell, keeping it closed."

"May I?" I need to know it's real and confirm his suspicions of it being sealed with magic. It's small and cool in my palm. The five-pointed star is beautiful in the dim glow of the tent and the ruby is perfect for what this represents. I turn it over, handling it with care as I examine the seal on one side and the small hinge on the other. There's a tiny hole, only big enough for a sewing needle to fit inside. "Any chance you have a needle?"

"No. Tailors and seamstresses usually handle all my fabrics." He answers and I roll my eyes at his snobbery.

"Fine. But it looks like you're correct. There is a small lock here and a needle would fit perfectly inside it. If you could allow me to hold on to this and when I get it opened, I'll give it back." I don't expect him to trust me with a family heirloom as powerful as this, but he shrugs and grants me permission. "Oh, and Lance? keep this between the two of us. You don't know who can trust these days."

"I trust you, Princess Gwenyfer." He looks at me the way any man with a crush would.

"Why?"

He approaches, reaching for me, but I step back. "Forgive

me, it's just you're very alluring. You demand attention the second you step foot in a room and your aura shines as bright as the sun. I know you are unwed and therefore I offer you this. When this war is over, we'll still need to align the courts. This is my proposal to become the king consort of Sagittarian Court."

I cup my hand over his mouth as I listen for my mate. Luckily, Arthur doesn't come in here and rip his head off for attempting to become my fiancé. "No offense, Prince Lance, but when the war is over, I intend to rule my Queendom without the requirement of a king by my side.."

I move my hand and he gives me a confused look. "You can't rule without a man. It goes against tradition."

"Fuck tradition and fuck the patriarchy. No one, not even a man, will stop me from taking my rightful place as queen. I hope you understand what it means to be my ally Lance, because if you try to come for me, my court, or my crown, the Scorpion Court will find themselves without a leader." I leave before he makes the mistake of agitating me further. Straight to mine and Arthur's tent where I find him setting up a picnic at the table. A small vase with two white roses is in the middle of our little table draped with a white tablecloth.

A plate of fruit and cheeses is on either placemat with a glass of wine to accompany it. "I can hear you standing behind me, Sunshine."

I walk up behind him, wrapping my arms around his waist and giving him a squeeze. We stand there for a few minutes as I find peace with him. "We have to leave."

"I know." He says. He spins around to face me before walking us backwards until he's sitting on the bed and I'm straddling him. "But we can stay in our little bubble for one more night."

I open my hand and show him the locket. "We have to open this and get the one back from my home."

"Are you sure it's still in the last place you left it?" He asks.

"Yes, but I'm not going to tell you and don't read my thoughts because the one thing neither of us will be able to do again is to see one another tortured. Knowledge is power, Arthur, and I don't want this to be one more thing Outher and his little witch shifter could want from us. He believes he has all the right relics, and right now, you and I know he doesn't. Diliha and Nefretiri should arrive tonight. I will speak to her then." His hands skim underneath my shirt, raising it so he can pepper my stomach with kisses. I sigh and let him consume my will to do anything but exist.

His fingers hook the waistband of my pants and slowly, expertly, he pulls them down until I'm exposed before him. "I think I'll make an appetizer out of your pussy before we eat lunch."

Arthur sucks on my clit and I grip his hair, pulling it hard. "You'll get no argument here so long as you keep doing that."

"Sit on my face, Sunshine. I want to watch you come undone while I feast on you." I remove my boots and the rest of my clothes. Arthur does the same before lying on his back. Then, I do exactly what he requested. His fingers dig into my hips and his tongue dips into my soaking pussy. I palm each breast and pick up a pace, riding him shamelessly. His sharpened teeth graze my skin, causing me to shudder, but I need more.

"More." I moan. "Please."

Arthur doesn't need me to elaborate as two fingers dive

into my pussy before he snakes his arm around and rubs the wetness around my ass. I arch my back and then he does something I wasn't expecting. He spins me around so I'm face to face with his thick cock already beaded with pre-cum. "Take my cock, Sunshine."

His hand slaps across both cheeks, the burn causing me to moan and push back against him. I wrap my lips around his head and suck, making him buck. I feel his tongue on my pussy again and his fingers finding my holes. As soon as I take him to the back of my throat, he plunges into me. Two fingers in each hole. I hold him at the back of my throat and let him take complete control of me. The power he has over me is exhilarating and what I need because outside of this tent, I have to take charge.

Arthur's fingers match his hips as he fucks all three holes, bringing me to my first climax. I scream around his cock. I want to feel him inside of me, so I move from on top of him with wobbly legs and instantly get back on him, placing the tip of him at my entrance with my back facing him and sink down. He sits up, his hands cupping my breast as his lips find mine and I taste myself on him. I ride him, using my fingers to stimulate my sore clit, but the pain and pleasure are what I want. "Fuck, you're so beautiful. I get to have you for all eternity, Gwenyfer. Ride me, baby girl, use my body in every way you want to."

Arthur's words of devotion have me clenching down on him and finding his lips, but I'm not done, and neither is he. I get on all fours on the bed. Arthur moves to the alpha position behind me. "Is this what you want, Sunshine? For me to dominate you? Make you submit to me while I fuck both your holes?"

"Yes." I moan as I push back, seeking him.

"Then put your hands behind your back." I do, and he ties a cloth around my wrists, pushing my face into the pillow. I turn my head to breathe as he leans over me, capturing my mouth before swirling his tip at my ass. "I love seeing my cum leak from all your holes, Sunshine, but most of all, this one. And this isn't even the extent of the pleasure I can bring you."

I want to ask what that means, but his dick claims me in one hard thrust as I bite the pillow to muffle my screams of pain and pleasure. He fucks me without restraint, causing bruises to pepper my skin as he brings himself to climax quickly pulling out watch his sees leak from me. But he doesn't untie me right away. I wait as a cool breeze causes a shiver to go over my exposed pussy in need of friction. The bed dips as he gets up. I watch as he cleans his cock and before showing me what he used on me before. "I know you love this, so while I fuck that tight pussy, your ass will take this. Can you handle it, Sunshine?"

"Yes." I moan.

The bed dips again as he positions himself to take me once more. The cool metal of the toy swirls my ass to lubricate it before he pushes it inside of me. "Hold on, Sunshine, because this time, I'm fucking you until I cum inside this tight pussy."

I'm sore but it's the best feeling in the world as he does exactly what he promised.

I awake to find Arthur dressed and sitting at the table. The sun has set and the cool night air drifts into the tent. He comes and kneels at my feet, love shining in those jade eyes. I kiss him deeply as I memorize his face. "We have something we need to discuss, Sunshine."

"Okay." I smile at the tone he is using.

"I've been coming inside you every time we've fucked, and while that's the best fucking thing I've ever experienced There's real consequences that come with it." He scratches his head and I see him afraid for the first time. "I don't think now is the right time to bring a baby into the world."

"I'm not ready to be a mother yet. You have nothing to worry about. I'm protected." His head hangs low as I see the physical relief in his shoulders. I grip his chin to make him look at me. "And one day, perhaps in five years when the world is safe, we'll have a daughter with eyes like her father's. If you were concerned, you could've and probably should've asked sooner."

"You're right, Sunshine. Except our baby girl is going to be as beautiful as her mother."

After we ate, I went to seek out Diliha, unsure if she had arrived yet. I heard hushed voices as I approached the headquarters tent. The regents from Tori and Diliha's courts having a conversation in hushed tones. One clearly aggravated with the other.

"Don't you see how well she controls that beast?"

"Yes, clearly the princess can do that. Who would've thought? Still, without all four pieces, we can't make the weapon that will eradicate them once and for all."

"Princess Victoria would still be alive if it weren't for those things. She'd be in agreement with us. Do you know where her locket is?" Princess Diliha's representative asks.

"The last I saw, it was on her when she left. I assume King Outher has it if the rumors about her death are, in fact, true."

"What about Prince Lance? He was acting kind of funny when we talked about them. Do you think he's lying?"

"Yes. We'll need to speak with him alone. Figure out what he knows."

"Is that wise? Going after a prince?"

"Do you think the shifter thought about that before killing Mauris?"

"No. I think there is something going on between him and the princess. He's rather protective."

"Well, she ran off with his brother. The one with blonde hair." I walk away, unable to stand their gossip any longer. The only good thing to come out of that eavesdropping was I learned that Tori more than likely had her relic on her when she was taken.

I make myself known before walking into the tent. It's dark, with nothing but a small wax candle flickering on the desk.

"Hello?" I call.

"Can I help you?" Lance asks, and I flinch as I spot him coming out of the shadows.

"Just wondering if Princess Diliha has made it here yet?"

"Ah, no, but this just arrived for you." He hands over a folded envelope. Sealed with her signature. I open it and read, my heart in my throat. I find myself losing another friend to Outher. "Something wrong?"

"Diliha and the Fae Chief have been taken by Outher's men." I reply. Her handwriting was messy, which told me she was in hiding as she was writing this in a rush. "Who brought this to you?"

"It was waiting on my desk when I came back after dinner. Didn't see who left it."

"Okay." Possibly fae magic. "Thank you. We should tell the others."

"Are you okay, princess?" He asks.

"Just fucking tired of Outher winning." I admit. "But he'll taste defeat soon."

"Have a good rest. We'll figure out a way to free them and all of Constellina in the morning. Tell that shifter to keep it down when he's fucking his next conquest. We could hear them throughout the entire encampment." I turn away from him before he can see the evidence of my embarrassment rise in my cheeks.

"Right. I'll pass the message along." I get out of there before he can put two and two together as I thought they all knew we were sharing a tent. But it's just like humans to think a royal would never sleep with one. Their loss.

When I get back in our tent, I find Arthur reading a book I didn't know he packed. It was worn, the spin creased, and the cover torn. I can't make out the title, but it looks like a thriller. "Anything interesting?

"Not since you walked in two seconds ago." He answers as he puts his book down, dog earring the page. I cringe. Books are meant to be loved, not tortured.

"I have some bad news." I take a seat across from him and hand over the letter. He skims it. "Yeah, but also some good news."

"My father really is a fool."

"Either that or Lettie is playing sides." I suspect. "Why would she pretend to use replicas of the stars, knowing they aren't real? And how is she still infusing shifter powers into humans?"

"Could be using one of her stolen fae tools. Those needles I told you about that extract magic, well they can do the opposite too." I bite my lip, trying to figure out the witch shifter, but drawing a blank. "I'm sorry that your friend got taken and the Chief, I actually liked her. But Diliha might have just given us the upper hand over my father."

He's right, of course.

"Well then, I guess we should start packing."

"Are you ready to go back home, Sunshine?"

Was I? I looked at my mate and knew that no matter what was thrown in our direction, we would come out on the other side hand in hand, or go down swinging. "Absolutely."

CHAPTER SEVENTEEN

Gwenyfer

The journey home wasn't long since the Fields are practically in our backyard. We move through the tree lines just as easily as I'd always done the many times I snuck out of the palace to admire the Wall of Illusion. Soon to be demolished by the magic Outher possesses. Even with fake ones, they have power. I don't know how or why, but I intended to find out, and there's one person who just might have the answer.

Arthur and I covertly make our way to the side entrance that Lord Regent never seemed to know about. It was one of the original servants' entrances, but over the centuries since this palace was built, it became abandoned. Other more convenient ways to come and go were developed.

The tunnel is dark and filled with cobwebs.

"Looks like no one's been down here in months." Arthur mutters.

"That's because I haven't been home in months."

"Right. How did you know about this, anyway? Secret hook up spot with passed lovers?" Arthur jokes.

"Of course. I used to bring servants down here for a quick fuck anytime I needed to blow off steam." His mouth gapes open at my serious tone. I bite my lip to keep my laughter in check. "Every one of them had something to offer their princess. There was one man in particular who could do glorious things with his tongue—"

"Sunshine," Arthur growls in warning, but I'm enjoying baiting him.

"Yes, he would kneel before me, look into my eyes, and run his ton—"

I don't get to finish my sentence as Arthur grabs me by my throat and pushes me into the wall. He presses his full body weight against me, running his tongue the length of my neck, making a whimper escape me and my pussy clench.

"You should've said no, Sunshine." He shoved his fingers into my pants finding my panties soaked through. With two fingers, he presses the fabric against me.

I pull him into a deeper kiss, my fingers skimming his hair. We break away faster than I wanted, but I know we're pressed for time.

We finally reach the end of the tunnel, and I open the door, peeking around the corner to ensure no one is nearby. Out in the corridor, I guide us to the stairs that lead to the upper level. There's no aroma of food like usual, nor the clanking of pots and pans. "Something's off."

"What?"

I walk into the kitchens. "It's too early for the cooks to have gone home." I swipe my finger across the counter, gathering dust. "And the maids haven't cleaned in here for a few days."

"Sounds like the Regent's been busy while you were away." He comments.

The next hall leads to the stairwell we take to the level where the throne hall is. "Two more levels and we'll be where the rooms are."

He nods as we keep going, but something is wrong. The palace is too quiet, and we haven't run into a single guard. My power crackles along my skin as I catch Arthur withdrawing his dagger from his boot.

I pick up the pace as we finally make it to my door. We go inside, the room is trashed. Furniture broken and clothes thrown astray. "You have a going away party?"

"No." I race to the hiding spot in the wall behind my broken vanity. Pulling a dagger from my boot, I use the hilt to dig the mortar out and pull the brick loose. I sigh with relief at the sight of the familiar brown box.

Back in my hands, I open it and then my heart sinks. "No. No. No! It's gone, but it can't be. I was the only one...fuck!"

"Looking for this?" I toss the empty box aside at the sound of that voice. "It's funny being the leader of this realm for years. I have my ways of monitoring everyone in this place." He walks inside, my locket dangling from his slim neck. Arthur stands at my side, ready to pounce if I say so. "Even the little princess."

"You're disgusting." I snarl. "Give it to me and I'll grant you the reward of a quick death."

"You won't kill me, princess. This relic protects me." To test that theory, Arthur throws his blade directly at the Regent, but it bounces off a force field. "What did I say? But you never were a good listener."

"There is a war going on. I don't have time for your games or petty issues. Give it to me unless you want Outher to enslave you."

"No. Outher would do anything right about now. Knowing that I can give him you, his bastard son, and the Golden Star." He sneers at us, but part of me thinks there's more to his scheme.

"You haven't sounded the alarms. Or attempted to capture us, which means we have something you want."

The Regent smiles and closes my door. "Even as a disobedient child, you were clever." He sighs, as if speaking was exhausting. "But I want something that only the two of you can give me."

"What's that?" I ask.

"You owe him nothing, Sunshine."

"She owes me this. If not for me, for her people, she abandoned me when she ran off with your brother." That was a jab at both of us. "Do you wish to listen to my proposal or not?"

"It's a trap." Arthur snarls under his breath, but something tells me it isn't. The Regent is scared.

"You want protection from Outher."

"I want a pardon. The freedom to live like a nobleman away from all of this royal bullshit."

"Why should I allow this?"

"Because you want this and the only way I give it to you is if you become queen." I look at Arthur and blink, unsure if this is a dream or nightmare. "By the markings on your arms, I say you found a husband. He's a prince, not human, but neither are you. Your birthday is next week. We announce the engagement tomorrow, send out invites, and bring the realm something to look forward to. To celebrate instead of fearing this war. You give the court the wedding of the century and take your place as queen and king consort. Outher will have no choice but to stand down."

"The people will never accept him as king." I argue.

"When we tell them it was how we negotiated peace with his king, they will. Plus, they have no choice. You'll have this relic and your husband. What does it matter?" the Regent fires back.

"It matters if the people will follow us. Respect us. I will not rule this Queendom through fear."

"You're a fool, Gwenyfer. Just like your father." I move forward, closing the large gap between us until I'm toe to toe with him.

"You don't ever mention him in front of me again. He'd have your head on a spike for what you and the Lirian Court plotted." His eyes flash with fear. "That's right. Alexxander told me it was the two of you who hired him to kill me."

"Yet here you stand."

"That's right, and once you hand over the relic, your knees will be the first to go. Then each digit, eyeballs, and I'll save your head for last. I want the entire world to know what you did. A traitor like you will garner no sympathy."

The Regent's eyes narrow. Then he gazes at me with pride, making me step back. "Spoken like a true queen. Give me what I want, and this little trinket will be yours. We'll call it a wedding present."

I don't break eye contact, but I feel Arthur's shoulder brush against mine. He leans over and whispers low-enough for only me to hear. "I'll agree to it, if it's what you truly want, Sunshine. And when you have that relic around your neck, those pretty jewels shimmering atop your head, I'll gladly grant you his death as a wedding present for my wife."

The last word comes out so smoothly it's as if it was meant for him to say. Of course it is. "Fine. You have a deal, but we vow it with blood. That way, if you even think about betraying me, you'll die."

"Smart choice. I'll begin getting everything ready. That staff will be delighted to hear that their princess has returned at last."

"Speaking of, where are the cooks?" I ask.

"I wasn't aware you went in for a snack before coming here."

"Guess you don't have eyes everywhere." Arthur comments.

The Regent sighs as he heads for the door. "I have moved the cooks to the new site."

"What are you talking about?"

"Let's call it a summer palace. It's where we've all been staying since a month after you were taken. Don't worry, they'll all be back in the morning." The Regent coos, and then he's gone.

There's a moment of silence before I look at Arthur, a shaky breath escaping. "I don't know what I'm afraid of most. That we'll be announcing to all of Constellina that I'm to wed, or that you'll be my king consort."

"We'll be fine, Sunshine. No matter what."

"There you go with being optimistic again."

"I may know how to say uplifting words around you, but don't forget the other ways my mouth influences you." He nips playfully at my ear, and I don't stop the smile from forming on my face.

"Tonight, we will rest, for tomorrow, the future truly begins."

Arthur

I've dreamt of leading an invasion into this palace many times over the years. It never once occurred to me that it's princess, soon to be queen, would be sleeping next to me with her head on my chest. Her soft skin pressed against mine after a deliciously hot shower session. Being king was never something I wanted. But for her, I'll do anything.

If tomorrow she wakes up, changes her mind, and says burn the fucking place down, I'll do it, no questions asked.

Her room was put back in order right after we ate dinner with the Regent. Gwenyfer was cautious the entire time. I could feel her turmoil through our bond, but a steady hand on her thigh had eased some of it. If I could take away every bad feeling, every ounce of pain she's ever felt, I would.

I press a soft kiss to her forehead before sliding out of the mess of sheets, the pad of my feet hitting the cool floor as I go over to the wardrobe to pull on some black pants. Out on the balcony, I look over the tree lines, past the wall, at the place I grew up. Where my life began, and my entire world flipped upside down. The day my mother died was the turning point for the Dracane Kingdom. He blamed Alexxander, then me, never once naming the person who was truly responsible for demise.

Soft fingers interlock over my navel as Gwenyfer presses herself against me from behind. She's slipped on a silk nightgown. For a while, we stand there, soaking in the warm night air while stargazing. It's the small moments of peace that remind me that the world isn't as fucked up as I thought it was. Correction, the moments with her.

"What are you doing up, Sunshine?"

"I could ask you the same thing."

I pull her around to my front, lift her to sit on the edge of the railing so we're at eye level and step between her legs. My grip on her hips is soft, but if she loses her balance, I know she won't fall. She smiles at me, her thumb rubbing across my cheek as I lean down to kiss her. "Are you sure about tomorrow?"

She nods. "It's quicker than we had discussed, although we haven't really talked about marriage. Regardless, my mind is set. The Regent is a sniveling little cock sucker of a traitor, but he made a valid point. With you standing by my side, we'll look united. Shifters will question why they're going to war and even the human armies."

"That's the assumption." I input.

"Arthur, what's truly eating at you about all of this? Ever since I told him I would agree to it as long as we sealed the deal with blood magic." It's funny how she thinks I'm dreading marriage when in fact it's the complete opposite. "I can see the wheels turning inside your head. Tell me and perhaps I can ease your discomforts."

She thinks I don't want this. That I'm not ready for it. I can't have her feeling like that. "To be honest, something about the way he showed up in your room was off. How did neither of us hear him? How did he know we were inside the palace when there was no one around? He's betrayed you before and I know he will do it again."

"That's why I said we use blo—"

"That doesn't always work. Thought you learned that when you made that deal with Alexxander?" I snap and her

182

eyes fall. Fuck.

"You're right. What should we do about it? To ensure that he doesn't run off to our enemies and divulge all our secrets? He won't give up the relic knowing it protects him." She slides forward, her feet landing on mine as I wrap my arms around her, pulling her to me. "What do you want, Arthur Penndragon?"

"Outher's head on a spike."

She smiles. "Then that is what I shall give you."

We kiss until I can no longer stand not being inside of her. In the middle of the night, she bent over the balcony with my cock buried deep in her. I fuck my mate until my name echoes on the wind and I have nothing left to fill her with. "When we're married, I'm going to fuck you every night over this railing."

"Oh, Arthur, you have no idea the places within these walls I'll take you. You might be the alpha when we fuck, but one day, I'll tie you up and show just how much you enjoy being my submissive."

The next morning, I was up before Gwenyfer, ready for us to eat and get this new plan started.

She dressed in pants and a pink blouse, securing her daggers to her thighs with straps she found amongst the destruction of her room. I stop her just before we head out to give her a few extra accessories. "I know you haven't needed them since your dragon took over, but," I pulled out a pair of pink-rimmed glasses and put them in place on her face. "I've always thought you looked beautiful wearing them."

"Arthur, how did you adjust the lenses?"

"There are none." I smirked, and she reaches up to feel that space. "I have one more thing." When she went back to sleep after our heated balcony session, I took it upon myself to dig through the mess that was her wardrobe where I spotted her jewelry box. That's when I found a piece of fabric, a torn part from a dress that was laced with gold and pink gems.

I worked tirelessly to get enough thread to create the one thing she deserves.

With her expression of appreciation staring at me, before I lose my nerve, I kneel and pull out the ring. "I know it isn't made from jewels, but it's the best I could do for our current circumstance."

"Arthur, you didn't need to."

"I know, but I wanted to and if I knew you would wear them, I would adorn you in all the gemstones of this realm. For now, this is what I have to offer. Gwenyfer, crown princess of the Sagittarian Court, will you do me the honor of becoming my wife?"

She said only six words before I slipped the golden thread ring around her left finger. "With all my heart, I'm yours."

The small rose quartz glistened the second it was secured around her finger. We walked hand in hand to the throne hall, where we agreed to eat and sign the papers with the Regent. When we entered, there wasn't much of a feast and that was because of the staff all trickling back in from the summer palace. The Regent was wiping oats from his mouth as we took our seats.

"What a lovely ring. Wherever did you find the time to get one?"

The Regent's question wasn't directed towards me, but I answer anyway. "I made it."

"Impressive. I didn't know you were a craftsman?"

"You don't know me at all." I snap.

"Well, it seems we'll be starting this morning off with a bang. Straight down to business I assume." He pushes his empty plate away and pulls a small stack of papers in front of him. "This is the pardon, marriage agreement, and necessary legal documents for when an heir rises to the throne. Now, I've listed a few potential candidates to be your advisor."

"I'll make my own decisions about who I want at my court." Gwenyfer states. "I don't care about the pen and paper stuff, Regent, we make this blood deal here and now before you cower and slink back to whatever grim infested home you crawled out of."

I love it when her authoritative side comes to life.

"So be it." Gwenyfer pulls out one of her daggers and a folded piece of paper. "You wrote it down?"

"Word for word. That way there's no loopholes." A mistake she made with Alexxander back at Locknite. "Every single one, in this order. Do not stray or I'll figure out a way to remove that relic and your neck from your shoulders."

I visibly see him swallow hard at her threat but his eyes skim over the sheet before he slits his hand and offers it to her. They connect, the hum of magic in the air as he begins to read:

"On this day, I William Von Dick, do solemnly swear to not betray, disseminate information, or speak a word against

Princess Gwenyfer of the Sagittarian Court. Even when she becomes the Queen. Her mate, Arthur Penndragon, will castrate me if I dare attempt to be disloyal to her or this court once again. Upon pain of death, I, William Von Dick, swear to never speak a word against her, her mate, the people of this court, and to bite my tongue until it bleeds if the urge to spill secrets surfaces."

I can't help but chuckle at the castration part.

"Finish it." Gwenyfer growls, her dragon coming to life in her eyes.

"And this deal is binding not only in blood but ink. The Golden Star shall be surrendered over to Princess Gwenyfer and that will be the last I ever see or speak on it. If I hear of any plot against the crown or the court, I am obligated to report it immediately. Otherwise, my hand will burn as a reminder of my oath." Dick, his new name, looks up from the paper and awaits Gwenyfer to speak her part.

"I, Princess Gwenyfer, do solemnly swear to grant you a pardon and absolve you of all your crimes. You may live the life you deserve." The clap of magic and flavor of ash fill my mouth as the deal is sealed between them.

"It is done." Dick says, and they sign the official paperwork.

William Von Dick made a deal with the devil, and she wears pink. My mate just ensured he would never see the light of day again, and I don't know if he even realizes it.

CHAPTER EIGHTEEN

Gwenyfer

After this morning's affairs, the rest of the day was filled with preparations for announcing the official engagement. Dick invited the Constellina News to cover the story and Arthur secured us some phones as another means of communication. I had to dress in a gown, make it look like the both of us were royalty. I was fidgeting with the corset when Arthur gripped my hand.

"You look divine, Sunshine. I haven't seen you in gold, but it fits the name I granted you."

"I hate it. Dresses and corsets. How do they expect a woman to fight in one of these?"

He laughs. "I don't think that's their purpose. But if it makes you feel better, I'll cut you off later, after I've had a small taste of your pussy."

I shudder as he skims a talon along my exposed shoulders.

"We need to go, and you have me wanting to fuck. How will I concentrate on the interview when you have me thinking about your tongue?"

"Hmm. I'll take care of you, Sunshine. I'm the trophy sitting next to you. Just paint that beautiful smile on your face and play your part." He presses a kiss to my cheek then whispers, "I'm going to have fun playing mine."

Before I can question what he meant by that, we're ushered forward to sit next to one another on a crimson couch across from a camera crew and news reporter dressed in a blue suit.

"Good afternoon, Constellina, I'm Bridget Miller reporting to you live from the palace in the Sagittarian Court. Today we have two very special guests, one presumed dead just a month ago. Turn your attention to crown Princess Gwenyfer and her new fiancé, Prince Arthur Penndragon of the Dracane Kingdom." There was a pre-recorded crowd clapping sound that one of the crew members played for a few seconds before she started with her first question. "Princess Gwenyfer, can you tell us what happened to you and where you've been these last six months?"

I adjust my glasses on my nose before coming up with my answer. "Well, I was in hiding."

"Can you elaborate? We were told that you were kidnapped, and then you ran off, abdicating your throne, then you died. But clearly, you're alive and preparing to become queen. The realm and all of us here at the news station would love to know what really happened." Her expression is laced with suspicion. Whatever I say next has to be believable, and the only thing that I can do is tell the truth.

I look at my mate, who offers an encouraging wink before holding my hand. His strength pours into me as our bond buzzes with life. We don't bother hiding our imprint, knowing that if asked, I will tell the truth. Any shifter watching will know what it means, and a thrill of excitement jolts through me at the idea of the entire shifter world knowing who Arthur's mate is.

I squirm in my seat at the feel of something caressing my thigh. It feels like a finger. I feel it again, moving higher until it's pressing against my underwear right over my clit.

Relax, Sunshine. I told you I'd enjoy playing my part. The people are waiting. Give them what they want while I take what I need.

Arthur, His invisible fingers push my panties aside and rub against my pussy. I cross my legs but could still feel him. "Princess Gwenyfer? Are you okay?"

I look at the reporter and let out a quick exhale before answering, focusing on my story instead of the talented fingers. "I'll start with the night of the ball when I was supposed to be engaged to Prince Mauris of the Lirian Court. Well, he never showed, and I was attacked by a rogue shifter. That's when Alexxander Penndra...gon." My breath hitches when Arthur's fingers press into my pussy and pinches my clit at the mention of his brother. They start at a punishing pace until I'm soaking and clenching. I feel his other phantom hand move to my ass, coating it with the wetness of my pussy before he fingers that hole.

"Someone bring the princess some water." Arthur demands, and a servant hurriedly brings a glass. I close my eyes while sipping on it, needing a moment before concentrating on the interview.

"The other prince rescued me and brought me to a place of sanctuary. After he told me of what happened, I stayed in

NOW AND FOREVER QUEEN

hiding until I could uncover who sent the shifter after me." I spit out.

Arthur.

I won't let you cum until you finish this interview, Sunshine. He adds his phantom tongue to the mix, licking and driving me crazy.

"And did you discover the traitor?" The reporter asks.

"Yes. It was Prince Mauris. He wanted me dead. Figured it would mean he could rule two courts instead of one. Alexxander Penndragon saved my life, but it didn't stop there. We were persecuted for the lies that were spread. King Outher sent assassins and his witch shifter Lettie after us. I spent time in Locknite Prison, but that's when Arthur and I met." His phantom parts pause for a moment as I look at him. "He saved me. And when I was freed, I spent the next three months' training and plotting my return to ensure we wouldn't bring war across the realm."

"That's when you two fell in love?" She asks.

"Yes. In a manner of speaking." I state. It isn't a lie.

"And now you two will marry to broker peace between the two realms?"

I smile. "It is what we wish for. King Outher is set on enslaving the human realm, but even if he doesn't agree to the terms of peace, Arthur will stand by my side as King Consort of the Sagittarian Court."

His phantom fingers and tongue pick up a heady pace. I'm close to oblivion, only a little more and I will be climaxing where I sit. "Prince Arthur, my next question is for you."

Arthur looks at the reporter, not giving anything away. While I close my eyes and focus on what I want to do to him. I imagine my mouth teasing the head of his cock, my tongue

190

running up the vein along his shaft. Arthur hisses as I opened my eyes.

I see you figured out how this works.

I do learn from the best.

Game on, Sunshine.

"Yes." It comes out steady.

Both of us turn our attention to the crew, while our phantom hands bring each other closer and closer to the edge. I'm nearly there and I can see he is too by the sweat gathering on his brow, the white of his knuckles from his tight grip on the frame of the couch. I can taste him on my tongue, feel him hitting the back of my throat. Just when I thought I can't want him more than I do at this moment, He pulled out of my mouth and somehow maneuvered his cock to where his fingers were just in my pussy.

I'm coming inside of all your holes before the afternoon is over, Sunshine. Even if it's phantom at first. I'm going to put you on your knees, my seed dripping from your mouth before I take your ass.

"Do you think your father will agree to a cease and desist?" Arthur looks stunned, but I know he isn't.

His gaze slides straight to the camera. Somehow, both of us know Outher would be watching. "No. Outher Penndragon knows only one thing, violence. The only way this world will ever live in peace is once he's six feet under and the worms are digesting his rotting corpse."

"You sound confident."

"That's because of who I am." Arthur narrows his eyes before continuing. "Outher, I know you're watching this. Good, because that means every word I speak won't be misconstrued. I challenge you to a duel to the death. Come to my wedding, enjoy the festivities if you must, but we'll end this war before it begins when one of us is dead. If you're not too much of a coward to face me."

I stop everything I'm doing. Withdrawing from our phantom session, and he does too. The atmosphere turns deadly serious with what he just did. "Princess, is this something you agree to? That the results of this duel, if the shifter king accepts, will decide the outcome of the war?"

I'm sure how to answer.

"Princess Gwenyfer and I have discussed this. King Outher will die by my hand. This way, no other blood has to be shed." Arthur answers and I sit united with him. To the crowd watching, we show them no fear in this rash decision. On the inside, I'm screaming at him.

"There you have it, King Outher Penndragon has two weeks to show his face. Or the courts will go to war." The reporter signs off and I stand, excusing myself to the private room that is behind the thrones. Arthur follows. Once the door is shut and the lock turns, I charge at my mate.

"How could you be so foolish? You didn't say a word to me the entire time you were teasing me with our bond." I scold him, my hands firm against him as I press him into the wall.

"It was a spur-of-the-moment decision. How did you expect me to think straight with those pretty lips wrapped around my cock?" He shoots back.

"Fuck you."

"With pleasure." Arthur's lips crash against mine, taking no time making good on his promise of tearing the dress from my body. In nothing but my boots, he tries to pin me to the floor, but I take over. Using the sash from my gown to bind his wrists and take control.

"I told you; you'd be the submissive. After what you just did, I deserve this. I will be the alpha this time." I bite into his shoulder, and he hisses.

"There's only one way to claim that position, Sunshine."

I used my fire to burn his clothes free of his body, and when he's fully exposed to me, I smile. Kneeling between his legs before knocking them wider. "I know."

His back arches the second I take him to the back of my mouth. Doing everything I did to him in that throne hall only skin to skin. Once I get his cock wet, I stand, walking over to the desk I sat at many nights before I was taken from this place to find my locked drawer. The only way in is with a code, and I know Dick wouldn't have any interest in this room.

I unlock it and smile when I find the lube and toy I used while fantasizing about my future husband. With the items in hand, I move over to him and his eyes widen. "Is the big bad shifter afraid of a little toy?"

"Bring it on, Sunshine." He looks at me with a challenge in his jade eyes. I pop the cap of the lube, coated the dildo before pressing the tip to his ass. "Fuck."

His Adam's apple bobs and I want this to be enjoyable for both of us. Turning around, my ass facing him, I sink down onto his cock and press the toy further into him. "Yes, take it like a good boy."

"Sunshine." He groans as I press it deeper before turning it on. "Oh, gods."

I ride him at the same time as I fuck his ass, finding it exhilarating having him at my mercy like this. His curses and moans, encouraging me to keep going. I feel the vibrations through him and desperately want the friction on my clit.

"Touch me." I demand and he snakes a phantom hand around my waist, finding my clit while I fuck him. My thighs burn as I feel the effect I have over him while his cock thickens inside of me. Then he explodes, his breath hitching as he nutted and his ass clenches around the toy. When he's finished, I pull the toy from him and get off his softening cock. But I'm not finished. I gently remove the toy from him, thoroughly clean it before returning with a wicked smile curving across my lips as I take my position over his face.

"My turn." He tries to break his bonds, but I shake my head. "Not this time, Arthur. I'm in control."

"Fine. Next time, I'm in control." He growls.

"We'll see. Open your mouth and don't forget to breathe." His tongue presses against my folds as I push the dildo into my ass before turning it on. I moan at the feel of both. I ride his face while fucking my ass, bringing me to my first climax.

I cut his ties, and he pins me to the floor, the toy still in my ass. His cock is hard again, and he doesn't hesitate to plunge inside of me. Not giving me a chance to recover. My ankles are at his head as he fucks me while using his other hand to punish my ass. "Arthur."

"Cum for me, Sunshine. I want to feel you milk my cock." So I do. Wave after wave, he brings me to climax. We continue on for as long as we can before we're both too sore to go on.

Lying on the remnants of my dress in a tangle of limbs, I run my fingers through his dark chest hair. "You should've warned me."

"I know. I'm sorry, but it was a last-minute thought."

"Will he answer the challenge?"

"I don't know. If he does, I'll be surprised, ready, but surprised." We were quiet, and soon I hear soft snores coming from him. I follow him into sleep because the next thing I know, the moon comes up. We'd stay inside this room all afternoon, a sacred bubble forming around us again.

"I've got you some clothes." Arthur says as I get to my feet to stretch.

"How?" I ask.

"Asked one of the maids that brought us dinner. Don't worry, she didn't see anything." He reassures me. "But if you'd like to bathe first, there is a robe and I'm sure you know another secret passage to get to your room from here. Did you really keep sex toys in here instead of your room?"

I walk over to him, putting the robe on. "Well, one can never be too sure who is watching. This room is warded against everyone except for the blood of the crown."

"Ah, I see. Your safest place to live out those tunnel fantasies." He queries, and I smile.

"We should get going. The next two weeks are going to be draining as it is." I say as he tucks a curl behind my ear and kisses me. "We'll survive this, Arthur. That I promise you."

"I know, Sunshine."

Arthur

The next two weeks were chaotic, as Gwenyfer said they would be. Interviews, dinners with other delegates, and even scheduling of fittings and balls. The one thing that hadn't happened was receiving word that Outher would be attending our wedding or accepting my challenge.

Tonight, I'll be attending my first royal dance as it's customary before the day of a royal wedding. I'm dressed in an all-black suit, my personal request. Gwenyfer would match me in her own way, and I was nervously waiting outside her room. When the door opened, my breath escaped me at the sight. She was wearing an all black dress with green flames sewn into the bottom of the skirt. Emeralds glitter from her ears and around her neck.

The golden tiara pinned to her hair is encrusted with pink gems to match her ring. "You're wearing our colors."

"Of course. You wouldn't expect me to wear anything else." She didn't cover up her arms, wearing our imprint with pride.

"I thought you hated wearing these things?" I ask.

"Good thing I'm going to be queen, and I can make custom orders." She lifts up the skirts of her dress to reveal her daggers strapped to each thigh. Then she took one of my hands and pulls it through a slit in the side. When my fingers make contact with her skin just above the hilt of her right blade, I can't help but kiss her. "We need to go, Arthur. We have plenty of time for sex later."

"Right."

We make it to the ballroom; the place alive with many people from all parts of the realm. I pull Gwenyfer close to me as we're greeted with false smiles and ample handshakes. When we finally reach the front of the room, Dick approaches us. "Everyone has arrived. All excited for the big day. How are the two of you faring?"

"I'd be happier if all these people left." I whisper.

"This is necessary." He claps back.

"Alright, has Outher arrived? Or any other shifters?" I scan the crowd at Gwen's question and spot a few familiar faces. All glamoured, but none were powerful enough to keep their identity from my dragon's eyes.

"Yes. And some are from different gangs in other courts.

None are my cousins, but some I recognize as followers of Alexxander." They wouldn't try anything in my presence, though. That I know for sure.

"How about a dance?" Dick suggests. Gwen looks at me, but before I can answer, the asshole orders the entire room to shut up and look at us. "Welcome to the celebration of Princess Gwenyfer and Prince Arthur. The gracious hosts would like to have their solo dance. "Clear the floor"

Gwenyfer takes my hand and leads me to the spot. "I don't know how to do this, Sunshine."

"Good thing I do. Just follow my lead." She places one of my hands on her hip and takes the other in hers while placing her free hand on my shoulder. I've seen others dance like this, but never had the desire to learn for myself. "Did they not have balls in your kingdom?"

"We had balls, Sunshine. Just not one's like this." Her brow raises in confusion. I smirk at her before whispering, "You had your mouth full of them the other night."

"You're so inappropriate." She laughs and the music starts. Nothing else matters after that. Everything around us melts away and all my focus is on the beautiful woman in my arms. She leads and I follow, spinning her when it feels right while keeping my eyes on her.

We dance in silence, our eyes and bodies saying more words than anyone could ever speak into existence. I'm so focused on her that I don't even notice the presence of another until his fingers hit her shoulder. "Might I cut in?"

"You showed?" I demand as I glare at the man partially responsible for my life.

"When you challenge me on global television, I'd be a fool not to." Outher huffs as he offers Gwenyfer a hand. "Let me enjoy a dance with my future daughter-in-law. Then we'll discuss terms."

"It's okay, Arthur, Outher knows what will happen if he tries anything." She says, but it doesn't matter.

"One single hair out of place and you'll fall on my sword faster than you can say the word oops." I warn.

"Understood." Outher nods. I don't like the way he is acting. His usual pride and anger isn't present. Something about him is different, as if he isn't the real man I know and hate.

I trust Gwenyfer and let them take the floor, keeping a short distance away as I focus on them. "Hello, brother."

Morgan stands at my side. "Come to kill my mate?"

"No. I have much larger fish to fry." I glance at her, she's wearing a crimson, tight fitting dress, matching our father's suit.

"Is Alexxander going to make an appearance tonight? Or does he still believe that I stole his mate?" If we're going to have a family reunion, I'm going to need whiskey.

"No." Her tone is coated in sorrow.

"What happened? Did he abandon you again?" Her tiny fingers grip my forearm as she pulls me away. "I'm not taking my eyes off him."

"Arthur, he won't do anything. I promise."

"I'd be a fool to trust you, sister."

"I need to speak with you." She waves her hand and creates an invisible barrier around us so no one can hear. "Alexxander isn't here because Outher thinks he's dead." I raise a brow, looking from her to Outher. "Father had Lettie take his magic."

"What?" That catches my attention.

"There isn't much time to explain, but Alexxander is mortal. I got him to a safe place before having to get back to Locknite. I don't know where he is now but I'm hoping it's far from this." She explains and I look for the lie, but everything in her gaze tells me it's true. "Lettie figured out how to harness the full extent of those fake needles. She stole his dragon. I watched her."

"Fuck. Why is he here?"

"He's here to challenge you before you step foot on the altar. Tomorrow morning, if you win, there is no war, but if he wins, Gwenyfer must become his wife. His consort."

"How do you know all of this?" I demand.

"I overheard him discussing it with Lettie. They've become closer." She grimaces with disgust. I don't need to ask what that meant.

"Why are you telling me this? He'll kill you for betraying him."

"Because I may hate your mate, but I don't like the idea of them taking our powers. If you kill him, Lettie will surrender. No more mutated humans, no more witchcraft."

The music ends and the pair make their way over to us. Morgan relinquishes the bubble and puts on a fake smile. "We have a lot to discuss. Is there somewhere private we can go?" Outher asks.

"Yes." Gwenyfer leads us to another room, not one we fucked in, but one actually used by Dick, who follows us inside.

"King Outher, what a great honor it is to have you here—"

"Enough with the pleasantries, Dick. I came here to answer the call." Outher interrupts. "Only it will happen in the morning before you can say your vows. You die, the crown, your mate, and this entire court is mine. I die, well let's just say I don't expect that to happen."

"You will die, Outher Penndragon, and the war will be over." I snarl.

"You accept my terms?" He forces his hand to mine. Gwenyfer tries to step in, but it's too late.

"I accept." Our deal seals with magic. "Tomorrow, I'll present your head to my mate before I become King Consort."

"We'll see." He sneers.

Back in our room, I wait for her to scream, but she silently gets into her night slip. I follow her lead as we slip into bed. When the silence becomes too much, I finally break. "Go ahead and yell, Sunshine."

"I'm not going to yell. No point in wasting my breath. Just don't die." I pull her close to me and kiss her forehead. "I'll be lost without you."

"I won't die, Sunshine."

"Promise?"

"Promise."

CHAPTER NINETEEN

Gwenyfer

"It's packed out there." I stare at the packed arena. It's different from when I trained for my own battles.

Arthur tightens his armor and secures his blades. They both got to choose a weapon, and he went with double swords. Their magic would be secured with iron bracelets so there would be no risk of a human being caught in the crossfire. He walks up to my side and watches as Dick announces the event of the day. We approach from the side, Outher doing the same with Morgan figuratively attached to his hip.

"You can do this. You have to beat him otherwise, I'll kill you." I warn while double-checking his armor. I didn't realize how nervous I am until he grips my frantically moving hands and pulls me in for a calming kiss. It's deep and I shouldn't think it will be our last, but I can't help but feel the small seed of doubt.

"I'll see you on the other side, Sunshine." Then I watch as my mate walks into the dragon's den to kill the man he once saw as his king and father.

Arthur

I've been here before.

Not with him, but with plenty others, and I've come out on top every time. The grip on my swords is leather, each blade perfectly balanced as I step up to the center, facing my father. He's chosen to wield double-headed axes. I remember him telling me that was what he was most skilled at when he was growing up.

It seems like a lifetime ago that we used to be close.

"The match will continue until one is dead. That is the terms of the agreement." Dick announces, then scampers back to the watch box where Gwenyfer and Morgan are.

"Surrender now, Arthur, and I'll let you and your mate go live a normal life somewhere far away from this realm." That's his tactic every time. Shit talking his opponent into striking first so he can assess which side they favor.

"A normal life? You mean a mortal one like you granted Alexxander?" His eyes dart to the stands, then back to me. "Yeah, she told me what you and that witch did."

"Your brother deserved his fate, just as you do." He snarls as he makes the first move. Striking for my right side, but I parry the blow, pushing him back a few feet. Outher recovers, but I'm ready for him to strike once more.

Our blades connect, each blow matched with strength and skill. I kick his favored right knee. He stumbles slightly, but I slice my blade across his torso, knocking the exposed part on the side. He bellows in pain as he turns on me.

He moves his eyes down to the bracelet and tries to break it off. It was a curiosity, but Gwenyfer ensured we'd be able to remove them in the event that someone tried to cheat. My dragon recognizes his eyes flashing over before we partially transfigured wings and claws. Tossing our weapons aside to fight like true beasts.

"I would've given you the world, Arthur. You were always my favorite."

"Liar." My fist connects with his jaw as he meets my gut. We stumble to the ground, sand flying all around us, coating my hair and hands. I have him pinned beneath me as I let a few licks go before he flips us and punches me with just as much force. He wraps his long talons around my neck, digging in deep enough for me to bleed, and my fire surfaces in my mouth. I let it go with a dragon's roar.

Green flames blast him a few feet off of me and I quickly jump to my feet. Outher is standing, his bones crunching as he transforms into a dragon with golden scales and crimson eyes. I look at Gwenyfer who shakes her head, asking me not to fight him in that form.

You can beat him. He's more exposed like that.

I look at my father's large figure. She's right. I'm a smaller target, which means he'll have to maneuver quicker to catch me. Scanning the ground, I grab my blades just as his jaws come close to my neck. I roll out of the way, landing on my feet before running under his belly, pointing the tip of both blades down the center of him as I go. His tail knocks into me and the wind is knocked out of my lungs as the crunching sound of my back impacting the wall reverberates in my head.

Outher's vast head is in front of me and with a dark look in his eyes, he blasts me with fire. His open jaws clamp down around my body, but I'm ready. Jabbing one blade into the roof of his mouth and the other piercing his tongue and lower jaw. He cries out, sparks burst from his throat until he falls backwards. I remove the blades and get out of his mouth before he swallow me.

Outher transforms back to his human form, blood dripping from his mouth and torso. His armor was discarded when he decided to fight me with magic. "Give up, Outher, and I'll grant you an honorable death."

"This fight isn't over." He races to his axes, and I meet him there, stepping a foot on one and bringing my knee up to his jaw. I spin out, my blades making contact with his forearms, severing the nerves and tendons, leaving them useless. With his back to me, I kick his knees in and he falls to the ground. When I step to face him, a menacing smile paints his face. "When I'm dead and gone, there will be an uprising, boy. Just know that without me, you, and you who—"

I don't let him finish his statement. My sword makes its final cut across his shoulders. Outher's head rolls and the crowd uproars with cheers as his body falls forward. His red blood painted the sand a deeper crimson color.

"Arthur!" Gwenyfer is in my arms faster than I can realize what just happened. Her lips meet mine in a frantic kiss as she pushes healing magic into me.

"I'm okay, Sunshine."

"Looks like we'll be having a wedding later. You two should get cleaned up. There will be time for celebrating at the reception." Dick states, and for once, I agree with him.

After I've showered and changed into the tux I'm wearing, the only color is the vibrant pink and violet rose pinned to my pocket, I look at my reflection, barely recognizing the man staring back at me. A knock sounds at the door as my sister enters.

"All cleaned up, I see." She fixes my collar.

"He needed to die.".

She nods, "I know, but he was still our father."

"And Alexxander is still our brother. We'll find him and figure out a way to help him restore his dragon."

"Well, since you're officially going to be king of a court, I guess you'll have more resources than a princess without a home." A tear falls from her eye, and I know it's not just for losing Outher, but our home, too. It will be destroyed without a leader. I am partly responsible for the misplacement of shifters.

"I'll talk to Gwenyfer, I'm sure if you pledge your loyalty to her, then you'll be pardoned for your crimes against her. She'll help us."

"I know. I knew her before you did." She sighs. "Let's get you married."

The ceremony wasn't a long drawn out one because

205

Gwenyfer ensured it would just be a few family members. Diliha and the Fae Queen made an appearance, as well as some of the other human court dignitaries. It was my sister who freed everyone from Locknite that didn't deserve to be there. Lettie however, is still on the run. My brother's essence is still in her possession.

"It's time for their first dance as husband and wife." Dick announces and I can't wait until the end of this long day so he would finally be out of our hair and the relic safe with Gwenyfer again.

"Actually, we'd like to skip that part. My husband has had a long day and we have some final matters to attend to before taking shelter in our martial suite." The crowd chuckles and I feel instantly relieved as her and Dick approach me. "Hand it over."

The former regent lifts the locket from under his shirt and hands it to her. She, in turn, gives him the signed pardon. "I hope we never see each other again."

"Are you sure you don't want me to kill him?" I whisper as he makes a swift exit.

"No. He knows what will happen if he betrays me again." She loops her arm through mine and guides me to the door. "Tomorrow is coronation day. We'll officially take our place as Queen and King of this court. Are you ready?"

When we make it to the hall, I push her against the wall and lean forward. "To worship you every night for the rest of my life?" I claim her lips, lifting her into my arms and running to the bedroom. She laughs as I kick open the door, toss her onto the bed and strip her bare. Once the door was locked, I burn my clothes and shoes off, crawling over her ready and not wanting to wait to be inside of her. I plunge into her soaking pussy, loving how she is always ready for me.

"I'm more than ready to be yours, my Queen. Every day for as long as you'll have me, I'm your body, mind, and soul." I claim each of her breasts, marking them before I begin a slow pace. We make love like the time we claimed our mate bond. Only this time was different. She wasn't just my mate, she was my wife and tomorrow, she'll be my queen.

CHAPTER TWENTY:

Alexxander

What could he possibly want from me now?

I make my way from the room I usually stayed in here at Locknite and make my way to my father's office. There are guards patrolling the halls and an unusual amount of activity late at night. I pull out my phone and notice the clock reads nearly midnight.

Insomnia is a bitch.

I knock three times until permitted to enter. On the other side, I see no one else in the room except him. Anxiety courses through me like a warning before a storm. I've never been here without at least my sister by my side. Do I fear King Outher? Only when he's in control of three of the four relics gifted with the powers of the gods.

"Sit down, Alexxander. There are some things I need

to discuss with you." He commands and I don't disobey. "Would you like a drink? You seem to be exhausted, perhaps a nightcap will help take the edge off."

"What's this about?" I ask, not wanting to deal with his attempt at breaking the ice.

"Your brother—"

"Not anymore." I interrupt. I stopped referring to him as family the second I saw his cock buried in my mate.

Outher scoffs, "No matter how much you hate him, you're still blood."

"Blood doesn't make you family." I stand, "With all due, little respect I have for you, Outher, if this isn't you telling me he's dead, then I'd really like to go back to bed."

He sips on his whiskey, eyeing me over the rim until I get the hint that he isn't going to convince me to obey him. I just have to listen. And that's what I do. "Good, I thought you might have been losing your will to live. Disrespect me like that again and you'll be in a cell next to him. Don't act like I forgot it was you who helped the little princess escape the first time. Pretending to be back in my good graces and all that. Ah, well we live and learn and that's exactly why I haven't punished you for that betrayal."

"Right. I've learned a lot over the course of six months." I mumble, meaning about mates and humans. Sides of me I never knew existed. I would've never given Outher the upper hand if she hadn't done what she did.

"Enough of this small talk," He reaches into his top desk drawer and pulls out a golden jewelry box. "Inside here are the weapons that will ensure the downfall of humans and put me at the top of the realm." I lean forward, growing interested as I suspect to know what he's hinting at. "Once your Aunt

Lettie has mastered them, there will be no more shifters versus humans because at the end of this pathetic war, there will be no humans left alive."

"You mean to kill them all?"

He shakes his head before answering, "No, why have a kingdom with no one left to preside over? I intend to turn them all into the one thing they hate most in this world." He pauses, giving me a chance to answer but I don't want to speak it into existence. Not that it stopped him. "All those pesky beings will become shifters. And when they figure out what gift I've granted them, they'll all fall to their hands and knees in worship of me. King Outher Penndragon of Constellina."

I'm momentarily speechless until I remember he asked me in here for a specific reason and it's not to hear his villain monologue. "What are your intentions for me?"

"You're going to be the control."

"What?" The doors open and five shifters, all carrying iron chains with gloved hands. I push to my feet, my dragon rising at the threat in front of me.

"You didn't think I'd let you go off and turn your back on me again, did you? No, you chose to bed a human, to free her when I specifically ordered you to kill her." I look at him in disbelief. Slapping myself for being a fool.

"Tell them to back away. There doesn't need to be any more bloodshed. I brought them to you. Gave you everything you asked for. I thought she was my mate, you should understand that more than anyone else." I protest.

"No. I'm done allowing my children to make decisions behind my back. Trying to use your mother's memories against me. If I am to rule over this realm, I must show everyone that you three will no longer be disobedient. Every choice has a consequence and sooner or later, they catch up to you."

"Eat your words, Outher. Because even if I can't stop you, she can. And that's why you really hate her. You're afraid of the little princess with shifter powers." His men charge at me, I get a couple punches in before they can subdue me in chains. I meet Outher's eyes and swear to him, "No matter what you do to me, Gwenyfer will be the one to kill you. It's been set in stone. And on the day of your destruction, no matter where I am, I will drink in celebration."

"We'll see how big of a game you can talk without all that dragon bravado to back it up." His words struck me. I played them on repeat as I'm being hauled off to a cell. On the other side is a room, much like the one they've been keeping Arthur and Gwen in. Only Lettie is waiting for me.

"You really should've become mine when you had the chance, Alexxander." She breathes out a heavy sigh, as if this is going to pain her more than me. "Strip him down to his boxers and secure him to the table. I don't want his dragon to realize what's happening before I can get the job done."

"What are you talking about?" I snarl, trying to rip myself free of the men but the iron burns my skin, paralyzing my powers. Every step, I headbutt, kick, and punch but nothing works as they cut my clothes from my body and chain me like a whipped dog. "You don't have to do this, Lettie. Outher is planning to eradicate the humans. Making a world–"

"Where shifters are the only creatures left? Yes, Outher has told me everything." She says with pride in her eyes. I recognize something more in them and I want to throw up at the images flashing in my head.

"You're sleeping with him? After all these years, my mother's memory, her friendship means nothing to you?"

She walks up to me, we're at eye level now. "I loved your mother but what my king wants he gets. Being a widow can be lonely at times. A good fuck is hard to find these days."

"And becoming his new queen has nothing to do with it?"

"It's just an added perk." She whispers. Leaning forward, her cherry painted lips brushing against my cheek before she says, "If you start calling me mommy, I promise I won't be mad."

I sink my teeth into her ear and tear at the flesh. She screams, stumbling backwards, anger bursting to life in her gaze. I spit the blood and torn flesh to the floor and snarl. "When I break free, you'll be the first to die."

Lettie rips open a box, takes out a leather pouch and unrolls it. From my angle, I see ten perfectly laid out needles, each marked with fae runic symbols. A lump forms in my throat because I know exactly what she intends to do to me. With her witch power, she raises five needles in the air, utter words of ancient fae, "lai-de-me su-e -far-nic." The sharpened points plunge into my skin, digging until they reach my bones. "When I have all ten inside, I'll take every ounce of your power."

"Outher doesn't just want to turn humans into shifters, does he?" I grunt out, unbearable pain coursing through me. The needles keep turning until they're locked in place.

"Not since discovering what these powerful little pricks can do." She raises the next four, and repeats the spell. The last one she walks over with in hand, placing the tip directly between my eyes before smiling, pausing a second. "Any last words before I make you mortal?"

"Take my dragon, witch, I don't need him knowing what is coming for the both of you." She laughs before jamming

the last point into the epicenter of the connection between my
soul and my dragons.

Morgan

Following Alexxander around all week wasn't something I
wanted to do but was demanded by order of the king.

He's so lost in his own mind that he still hasn't noticed
me. We don't talk like we used to and sometimes I miss
those conversations. We were good before that bitch princess
showed up and ruined everything. I get pure enjoyment seeing
her day in and day out feel the pain of Arthur getting tortured.
That's the consequence of finding your fated. When they die,
a piece of you goes with them.

It's been six days since we captured the traitors and I've
been waiting for something more exciting to happen. He has
three of the four relics, why not just use them already?

Alexxander's door opens and I look at the time.

Why are you up so late? I should be in bed too, but I
overheard the guards whispering that Outher would be
summoning him. Which meant I would be too, yet it hasn't
happened yet. I follow behind him, keeping my distance as he
makes his way to the office. In my many years coming here,
I found the perfect room with a vent I can use to listen in on
everything going on. Sometimes, I've regretted eavesdropping
on Lettie and Outher. I shiver at the memory of those sounds.

Listening in on this conversation took a darker twist
than I ever expected. I quickly follow as the guards brings
Alexxander to Lettie's personal torture room. Her dark magic
is the only reason Outher has kept her around all these years. I
slip inside just before the doors close, waiting in the shadows
using my glamor to melt into the wall. She'll never see me,

and Alex is the only one who knows of the unique gift I have. Some dragons a long time ago were able to camouflage their surroundings. My scales cover my false skin, matching the cell perfectly.

I watch in horror as Lettie begins to use those tools on my brother. For fear of losing my own dragon essence, I'm paralyzed. Each turn of the needle, his eyes flashing over, growing dimmer and dimmer until the last of his flames are put out.

"Mak-de par-te -fri-de." The power suckers withdraw from his skin, blood pooling down from the open wounds as she brings them all together in a bundle. Placing them in a crystal jar and uttering more ancient words I'll never understand. Golden swirls of light flow out of the needles and into the jar. "You see, Alexxander, if you would've just stayed by your father this piece of you, would still be on the inside. Your dragon was one of the more powerful ones. Now, it will be used to make more shifters."

I look over at my brother, he's unrecognizable. Muscle mass deflated, skin pale, and sweat mixes with his blood. If I don't heal him soon, he'll die. When I go to move, I halt when the door swings open and my father walks in. Lettie bows her head, jar of essence in hand, and presents it to him like a doctor showing a mother their newborn.

He takes it and smiles, "So this is what our essence truly looks like?"

"Yes, my king. It matches whatever our scales and or fire would be."

"And this is all of it?" She nods. "Good. Heal his wounds then throw him on the outside of Locknite. Let's see if he can make his way out of the desert lands without dying as a mortal human first."

I wait until Lettie and my father leave to go have a celebratory fuck. When we're alone, I rush over to him, lifting his head up only to find him unconscious and barely breathing. "Alex, wake up. You have to stay alive."

"Stop…" he mutters.

I hold the heavy weight of him and press my hand to his wound. Pushing power into it, I seal the first one closed. "Alex, come on, you need to listen to me." I slap his face, not hard, to try and wake him. His eyes flutter open and close until he sees me. "I'm not going to let you die as a human. I'll find you; I promise."

The sound from approaching guards has me quickly healing the rest of him and then melting back into the far wall. I watch with my heart in my throat as they drag his near lifeless body away.

Back in my room, I rummage through my things for a bag. Then race across the hall to Alexxander's room, going through each draw and finding clothes, shoes, and a weapon. He carried none as typical for someone who has a powerful dragon at his beck and call. Only he's mortal now and will need protection. After filling the bag with some supplies, I make my way to the pantry, place non-perishables inside, then go to the armory and find a small switchblade he could use. The only thing left would be his phone. Which was in the pile of discarded clothes.

I make haste and go to the incinerator but I'm too late as all the trash has been burned for the day.

"Fuck!" I slam my fist on the table and then look at the time. Pulling out my own phone, I quickly unlock it, take the password off and place it inside. Racing around the halls, I sneak my way down to the lower level and just catch up in time to see them toss my brother outside. I wait until it's clear before making a swift exit. My wings burst from my back, and I lift him into the air, determined to get him to safety before Outher and Lettie finish their dance within the bed sheets.

I get as far as the sands meet the grass, and find a shady spot to put him down. Setting up the tent I packed and caring for him as he continues to go in and out of consciousness.

"We'll meet again, Alex. For now, this is all I can do." I kiss his forehead and then rush back to Locknite before anyone realizes I was gone.

Alexxander

I'm drowning in a sea of darkness. My lungs constrict as I try to breach the surface.

Something cold pressed against my forehead and I reached out for the hand calling to me.

My eyes flutter open and in the light of the sun, I see chestnut eyes staring down at me. "Easy, big fella, you've been fighting off a nasty sickness for weeks."

I look around and notice I'm in a healers wing. "What... how...who?"

"Confusion is a common symptom when one is in a coma. You were brought here about three weeks ago by someone who said they found you on the brink of death in your tent. Must have caught something when you were camping. Do you happen to remember your name?" The woman asks and I furrow my brows.

I try to recall who or what I am, but all the images are blurred. "I'm not sure. I can't remember."

I wince as I try to sit up. "Here, drink this tonic. It should give you instant pain relief."

It's a mixture of sweet and sour and I nearly gag on it. "Thank you..." I look at the button clipped to her white dress. "Lara."

She flashes me a quick smile, "You should be able to go home in a few days. All your infections are healed but your body is weak. We've only been able to feed you through that tube connected to your arm, but, if you're feeling up to it, I'd like to give you solids."

"Sure." I guess that was the correct answer as she left and came back with a tray of jelly and creamed potatoes. "Why do I remember everything except my name and where I come from?"

She shrugs, "Most coma patients remember things slowly. Some not at all. It all depends on what your triggers are. If you've forgotten who you are and where your family is, then whatever happened to you is a result of a trauma related incident involving them. I apologize and give you my condolences if that is the case."

"Will I ever remember?"

Lara perks up, grabs a spoonful of the red gelatin, and holds it up to my mouth. "I will work with you until you do. Even after you're discharged. If you want it."

I swallow the strawberry sweetness and smile. "Considering you're the only person I've met, then yes. I would appreciate all the help I can get right now."

"Good. Now, eat up and later we'll get you up on your feet."

My recovery took a lot longer than anticipated. I couldn't stand on my own without a walker to help me for three more days. The food portions grew slightly more with each meal but after I threw up the first night, Lara grew concerned and we took it slow again. She assisted me in a shower, saying sponge baths were only good for so long. When she pulled the catheter out of my dick, I howled like a dog. Her reasoning for it was so I wouldn't piss myself.

She was kind and easy on the eye. Her body had all the perfect amount of curves I could sink my teeth into. Something about this woman made me feel like a man again.

"Not like that you buffoon." She ridicules me as I try to relearn how to use a phone. One that she said was in my backpack. "This is how you use an emoji."

Lara sent a smiley face image to herself. "Why do I need to use these things?"

"Because it's modern and you can say a lot with one little picture."

"Right." I don't quite understand. "Am I truly leaving today?"

"Yes. I've set you up in the guest room of my house."

"What? No, I don't want to intrude. Besides, you've been with me since I arrived here. You've done more than enough." I try to argue with her, but Lara is like a brick wall. Stubborn and hard-headed, when she sets her mind on something, there is no point in trying to persuade her of the opposite.

"Just pack your bags and take a shower. I don't want you stinking up my house on the first night." I laugh and watch as she walks away, my attention ensnared by the sway of her hips.

Lara Dean is exactly what I didn't know I needed.

The story continues in book three of World of Constellina Series: Alexxander & Lara Dean's story

In the midst of the war-torn courts of Constellina, undercover Princess Lara Dean finds common ground–and heated passion—with her patient, unaware that he is the twin of her mortal enemy that slayed her brother.

STAY IN TOUCH:

Instagram: @cerahano
TikTok: @cmhano_author
Twitter: @HanoCera
Facebook: C. M. Hano
Facebook Reading Group: C. M. Hano's Reading
Warriors
YouTube: The Literary Works of Cera Hano
Linktree: https://linktr.ee/cmhanoauthor

Scan the QR Code for more information:

ACKNOWLEDGEMENTS

First and foremost, I would love to thank my husband Philip and my two daughters, Kaylee, and Abigale, for always supporting me in this dream. Without your patience and sharing of me with my computer, I wouldn't be able to put these stories to paper. To my parents for their continued support, especially my moms who read everything I write, to include all the spicy scenes. To my alpha and beta readers, thank you for the encouraging and crucial feedback I get on a daily basis. Without your honesty, I would be lost in the bias of my own work. To Charly and Sue, my editors, and formatters for making the final piece of this work polished and always having my book babies in their best interest.

Finally to you, the reader, who continues to support me in this endeavor. I truly hope these stories and characters touch you in a way they do me.

ALSO, BY C. M. HANO

YA-Fantasy
The Princess Chronicles
The Journey Begins #1
The Hollow Realm #2
The War Back Home #3

LGBTQ NA-Fantasy
TarotVerse
Xora #1
Whitfrost #2

Sci-Fi NA-Fantasy
The Cursed Parlay
The Cursed Parlay #1
Across The Starless Sky #2

Reverse Harem Fantasy
World Of Zavinia
Queen of Kings-Prequel
Fate Awakens #1

NA-Fantasy

World of Constellina
Once and Future Queen #1

Now and Forever Queen #2

Ruthless Royals
Fated Assassin #1

The Huntress Saga
The Huntress #1

PNR-Standalone
Night & Day